"What do you really want for Christmas, Brandi?"

Zack continued, "Emeralds? They'd look good against that auburn hair and fair skin of yours."

"I hardly think Santa's likely to bring me emeralds."

"Well, that's true—at least *this* Santa. We hardly know each other, so it wouldn't be proper for me to give you jewelry."

This, Brandi thought, is getting out of hand! "I can't think why you'd need to know, anyway!"

Zack frowned. "You're not just unromantic about Christmas, are you? You're downright oblivious!"

Leigh Michaels has always loved happy endings. Even when she was a child, if a book's conclusion didn't please her, she'd make up her own. And, though she always wanted to write fiction, she very sensibly planned to earn her living as a newspaper reporter. That career didn't work out, however, and she found herself writing for Harlequin Mills & Boon instead—in the kind of happy ending only a romance novelist could dream up!

Leigh likes to hear from readers; you can write to her at P.O. Box 935, Ottumwa, Iowa, 52501-0935, U.S.A.

Books by Leigh Michaels

The Unlikely Santa
Leigh Michaels

Harlequin Books

TORONTO • NEW YORK • LONDON
AMSTERDAM • PARIS • SYDNEY • HAMBURG
STOCKHOLM • ATHENS • TOKYO • MILAN
MADRID • WARSAW • BUDAPEST • AUCKLAND

ISBN 0-373-03388-5

THE UNLIKELY SANTA

First North American Publication 1995.

CHAPTER ONE

BRANDI Ogilvie was not having a good day.

A shipment of Christmas supplies—twinkle lights, wrapping paper, and tree ornaments—which had been promised for delivery that morning had gotten lost somewhere between the warehouse and the store, and Brandi spent the better part of two hours on the telephone trying without success to track it down.

A sudden, virulent flu had taken out a half-dozen workers in the course of the morning and was threatening to decimate her staff before the week was out—hardly a cheerful thought for the first Monday in December. It was the crucial second week of the Christmas shopping season, and the Tyler-Royale store in Oak Park, Illinois, was a major department store, not a self-service discount outlet. As its manager, Brandi needed every person she could get on the sales floors.

And as if all that wasn't enough for one day, her secretary paged Brandi away from her lunch break before she'd eaten the first half of her hot pastrami sandwich. She sighed and picked up the other half to take back to her office, and as she was leaving the tearoom, two youngsters who were playing tag around the tables crashed into her. Mustard squirted from the sandwich over her new cream-colored silk blouse.

"Urchins," she said under her breath. "What are they doing in here anyway? And where are their parents?"

Brandi didn't expect an answer, and she was startled when a voice at her elbow murmured, "Right over there, drinking coffee and peacefully oblivious to their children's antics.'' Casey Amos, the department head of ladies' active wear, reached past Brandi to pick up a linen napkin from the nearest table.

Brandi took it and dabbed at the stain on the front of her blouse. ''I'd like to ban kids from the tearoom altogether. That's why we put in the cafeteria downstairs, you know.''

''You'd feel better if you sat down and ate something reasonable,'' Casey diagnosed.

''It's got nothing to do with where and what I eat. It's the season. Just between you and me, I hate Christmas, Casey.''

''Now is that a proper attitude for the manager of a Tyler-Royale store? Don't you remember what Ross Clayton said at the sales conference just last week?'' Casey struck a pose in imitation of the chain's chief executive officer and deepened her voice. ''Always remember Christmas is the engine that drives retail sales. We'll do a third of our year's business between now and New Year's Day. And every single one of our customers is apt to walk through our doors in the next six weeks. Catch that customer and keep him or her happy!''

Brandi feigned a frown. ''Does that mean you think our beloved leader would object if I spanked the brats?''

''Darling, I doubt you could catch them,'' Casey said frankly. ''If you were eating properly and taking your vitamins, I'd put money on you, but...''

Brandi laughed. ''All right, I'll order a salad next time. I suppose this serves me right for being in such a hurry—I shouldn't carry food around.''

She could hardly go back to work drenched in mustard; her secretary would just have to be patient for another few minutes. Brandi stopped in Salon Elegance, the department that handled upscale women's clothing, and bought a duplicate of her blouse.

The clerk charged the sale to Brandi's Tyler-Royale credit card and offered to send the original blouse out for cleaning. "It may be too late already, Ms. Ogilvie," she said. "Mustard's a tough one. But we'll do our best."

Brandi pinned the white carnation that marked her as a manager to her shoulder, gathered up her receipt and wallet and made a mental note to compliment the woman's supervisor about her helpful attitude. Then she headed for the escalator and her office. She was feeling much better, now that she was properly dressed again.

Christmas was just a state of mind anyway—in less than four weeks the holiday season would be over. She'd survive the pressure this time just as she had for the past half-dozen years. It was simply part of the job. And someday, when she moved farther up in the corporate structure, she wouldn't have to deal with this sort of pressure around the holidays.

In Tyler-Royale's anchor store in downtown Chicago, the executive offices took up two whole floors, but in the rest of the chain—even the big suburban stores like this one—space was precious and managers made do with much smaller quarters. Brandi's office lay at the end of a narrow corridor on the top floor, cramped between the employees' lounge and a storeroom, and her secretary's desk occupied a tiny alcove just outside her door.

The secretary looked up with obvious relief at seeing her boss. No doubt, Brandi thought, that was because today the alcove seemed even smaller than usual—the single visitor's chair beside Dora's desk was occupied.

"Sorry I took so long, Dora," Brandi said briskly. "I had a little accident and had to change my blouse. Have I forgotten an appointment?" But she didn't remember scheduling a supplier or a sales rep today, and Dora usually let people like that sit in her office rather than subject them to the cramped alcove. So who was waiting for her?

The man rose with an easy, athletic grace Brandi couldn't help but admire. She was tall herself, but her nose was on a level with the knot in his tie—a black tie, over a white shirt, under a V-necked sweater in a bold black-and-white pattern. His eyes were almost black, as well, or was that just the effect of the dramatic clothing? And his hair was black; it looked silky and fine and soft.

Dora said, under her breath, "He's waiting for you, Ms. Ogilvie. He says he's your new Santa."

Brandi blinked and looked up at the man again. Mid-thirties, she estimated. There was not a strand of silver in his hair; his shoulders were broad and his stomach perfectly flat, and his face—though far from unpleasant to look at—was too well chiseled to be called merry. His was hardly the sort of physique she normally sought for the job; this man looked more like a model—the rugged, outdoor kind—than a stand-in for jolly old Saint Nicholas.

Furthermore, Brandi thought, he ought to have realized that much himself—unless he was suffering from some kind of delusion. Maybe he really thought he *was* Santa Claus?

"Did you call security, Dora?" she asked softly.

Despite her low tone, the man heard her. "No need for that, Miss Ogilvie."

His voice was low and warm and rich and reassuring; that much was exactly right for the part. But the rest of him...

Dora shook her head. "He didn't seem threatening, exactly, just determined."

Brandi didn't have any doubts about the determination. She turned to face the man. "It's *Ms.* Ogilvie, please. And if you're looking for a job..."

His eyes dropped to her left hand, where a diamond cluster sparkled on her ring finger, then met hers again, without hesitation. "It's not a matter of looking, exactly, Ms. Ogilvie, I *am* your new Santa."

Brandi said dryly, "You'll pardon me for not recognizing you. Perhaps it's because you're out of uniform?"

His smile started in his eyes, she noted. It was quite a nice smile, slow and easy; it lit up his whole face and showed off perfect teeth and an unexpected dimple in his left cheek.

Dora cleared her throat. "Also, Ms. Ogilvie, there's a call for you from Mr. Clayton." She said the name with the same reverence most of Tyler-Royale's employees used when referring to the chief executive officer.

Brandi frowned a little. "And you've kept him waiting? Why didn't you tell me that right away?"

"He said not to disturb you, that he'd wait till it was convenient."

Brandi's frown deepened. That didn't bode well; Ross Clayton was a good and thoughtful employer, but it wasn't like him to be so very considerate of his manager's schedules. "I'll take it right now," Brandi murmured and turned back to her unlikely Santa. "Hiring isn't my department anyway. Perhaps you'd best speak to the personnel director—third door down the hall, on your right." Without pausing to see whether he obeyed, she closed her office door behind her and picked up the phone. "Ross, I'm sorry to keep you waiting."

"It's no problem. This is in the nature of a favor, so I didn't want to disturb your lunch."

"Don't let it worry you. You'd have been the least of the disturbances. What can I do for you?"

"I'm sending a man out to see you this afternoon."

Brandi closed her eyes. "Very tall?" she said warily. "With black hair and a grin so charming it almost makes you overlook the fact he's a maniac?"

"That sounds like Zack. He's showed up already, has he?"

Brandi rubbed the bridge of her nose. "Oh, he's here."

"He's generally on the ball. Good, you can put him to work right away. I know you can always use an extra Santa."

"With all due respect, Ross, I don't need another Santa. I have three perfectly good Santas hired already. Their work schedule is set up through Christmas Eve, and..."

"I hear the flu's getting really bad. What if you lose one?"

"That's why I've hired three. Ross, they're all honest-to-goodness grandpas, with real white beards and real white hair. They're even just about the same height so they can swap costumes. Tell me, where am I supposed to get a Santa suit for your Goliath? Besides, those kids are a tough audience. I can't just stick a couple of cotton balls on your friend's face and make him look believable!"

"I know you're a stickler, Brandi. But as a favor to me..."

Brandi wanted to groan. "Let me guess," she said crisply. "He's an old friend of yours who's fallen on hard times, and you're finding him a job?"

"He's got some problems just now," Ross agreed.

"That figures."

"It's only a seasonal job, Brandi. Just through Christmas."

"I don't need a Santa," Brandi muttered. "I need an assistant manager and another six clerks who can float to any department."

"What?"

"Never mind. Is this a direct order, Ross?"

"Brandi, you know I like to give my managers maximum authority. I try never to issue direct orders in matters that affect a single store."

"That means it is. All right, Ross—your Santa has a job." She put down the telephone and dropped her head into her hands for a few seconds. Then she punched the intercom. "Dora, is Santa still out there?"

"Yes." The secretary's voice was little more than a whisper. "He won't leave."

"I'm not surprised. Send him in."

Brandi sat at her desk and watched him as he crossed the narrow room and took the chair opposite her. He moved like an athlete, perfectly at ease with his body and in command of every muscle. She wondered if he was a dancer, too—there was something about the way he moved....

As if it mattered, Brandi reminded herself. She eyed his cable-stitched sweater and houndstooth-check trousers. He wore his clothes with an ease that said they weren't brand-new, as she'd half expected them to be. So Ross hadn't fitted his friend up at the downtown store before sending him out to Oak Park. And his clothes were expensive; Brandi had no trouble recognizing the quality of the whole outfit. Whatever hard times this man had fallen on were obviously recent ones.

She picked up a pen and doodled a square on the edge of her desk blotter. "Ross said your name's Zack?"

"That's right. And I'll happily let you call me that if you tell me your first name in return."

Brandi looked at him levelly, eyes narrowed. "Don't be impudent. I may have had to give you a job, but I don't have to make it easy for you."

He bowed his head. Brandi couldn't help but feel the submissive gesture was tinged with a good deal of irony. "Zack Forrest, at your service."

"That's better. Mr. Forrest, I'm sure you understand that Ross doesn't assign entry-level jobs in his stores. That's up to the managers. And right now I don't need a Santa. What I could use is floor help—clerks who float throughout a department and assist the customer to find what he or she wants. If you're interested, I can put you down in men's active wear this afternoon for training, and—"

He was shaking his head. "Ross sent me here to be a Santa."

"I just told you . . ." Brandi paused. "Look, I'm sure Ross meant well. But he doesn't know what's going on out here."

Oh, that was great, she told herself. The last thing she needed was for Ross Clayton's friend to go back and tell him that the manager of his Oak Park store said he had no idea what was going on!

"I want to be a Santa," Zack Forrest said. "In fact, I insist on it." If his voice hadn't been so deep, Brandi would have sworn he sounded like a stubborn three-year-old.

"Or what?" Brandi said in disbelief. "You'll report me to Ross? I don't know what kind of hold you have on him, but—"

"I wouldn't call it a *hold*, exactly," he said thoughtfully.

Brandi gave it up. "Why did he send you to me anyway?"

Zack shrugged. "He said this store has the busiest Santa's Workshop of any Tyler-Royale location."

"That's partly because I'm so careful who I hire to man that department." Brandi paused and thought, I can't believe I'm explaining my hiring practices to him!

He treated her to another slow, unrestrained smile. "I thought you said hiring wasn't your responsibility, Ms. Ogilvie."

"You know, with that kind of attitude it's no wonder you're out of a job." Brandi stood up. "You can report to the personnel manager and fill out the paperwork. Be sure to leave a phone number. Since it will take some time to find a Santa suit your size—"

Zack Forrest had risen, too, and Brandi let her gaze run from his face to his well-polished black wing tips and back, hoping the curt appraisal would take him down a notch. But he didn't even blink, just stood quietly and watched her face while she looked him over.

Brandi went on, "We'll be in touch when we can put you to work. Don't expect a call for a few days, though, because I'm sure finding a suit to fit you will be—"

"No problem at all," Zack interrupted. "I happen to have one in my car right now. I can go to work this afternoon." There was a glint in his eyes. "If you like, that is."

Brandi was taken aback. "Fill out the paperwork first and we'll see," she said finally. "I'll call the personnel director and tell him you're on the way."

The corner of his mouth quirked as if with satisfaction, but he didn't say a word till he was at the door of her office. Then he paused and turned. "You owe me one, though," he said gently.

Brandi had already picked up the telephone. She looked up from it, her mouth ajar. "One what? Listen, buddy, if you think you're the one who's doing *me* a favor here—"

"Oh, no. I appreciate everything you've done for me." There was a faint note of irony underlying that rich, warm voice. "I just mean I've earned equal time to look you over as thoroughly as you've studied me, Ms. Ogilvie."

"I beg your pardon?"

"And I reserve the right to do so... someday." He sketched a salute and pulled the door closed behind him.

Brandi sank back into her chair. At this rate, it was going to be a very long time till Christmas.

Brandi couldn't settle to anything constructive that afternoon, because the face of her unlikely Santa kept popping up between her and whatever she was trying to do. Finally, she pushed all her paperwork into a desk drawer and went out to do her daily tour of the store.

Early in her training, Brandi had learned to pop into every department frequently but unexpectedly, just to be certain her staff was performing up to specifications. It had turned out to be a good habit; in her two years as manager of the Oak Park store, Brandi had avoided a lot of big trouble by catching problems while they were still small enough to handle. It was one of the reasons that her store consistently ranked near the top of the Tyler-Royale chain when it came to profitability.

Though if the CEO kept sending her employees she didn't need or want, her record was likely to be chipped away. What had gotten into Ross Clayton anyway? Zack Forrest had denied having any hold over him, but Brandi didn't believe it for a minute. It just puzzled her to think what it could be.

Mondays were always the least hectic day of the week in the retail trade, but already this was shaping up to be the busiest Christmas season Brandi had ever experienced, and despite the day the store was comfortably full of shoppers. Some were admiring the long double row of decorated trees that lined the atrium entrance, inviting the public to come in for a closer look. Others were already heavily loaded with bags and boxes in Tyler-Royale's trademark blue and silver. In the toy department, several women browsed, and nearby a line of children waited to reach the big chair that sat just in front of the elaborate facade of Santa's Workshop.

Wait a minute, Brandi thought. There wasn't supposed to be a Santa on duty this afternoon—not till evening, when children were out of school and families came to shop.

She paused at the railing that surrounded Santa's Workshop and helped to keep the line orderly in particularly busy times. This wasn't one of those times; at most, a dozen children were waiting to talk to the man in the red suit who sat comfortably in the throne-size chair with a child on each knee.

Brandi went to the nearest checkout station and called the personnel director. "Did you assign our new Santa to work this afternoon?" she asked bluntly.

The man sounded stupefied. "Of course not. I gave him the employee handbook and said we'd call him when we got the schedule straightened out, just like you told me to do."

"That's what I thought," Brandi muttered. She put the phone down. By the time she got back to Santa's Workshop, the two boys had gotten off Zack's lap and a little girl had climbed up.

Brandi leaned against the rail and watched for a moment. She had to admit that Zack Forrest made a better Santa than she'd expected. Despite some padding around the middle, he was still a bit on the lean side, and Brandi could tell from across the room that his beard was fake. But he'd brushed something into his eyebrows to turn them gray, and his suit was perfect—the heavy red velvet was trimmed in what looked like real white fur. And he hadn't settled for cheap black patent accessories, either—this Santa's belt and boots were top-grain black leather, polished to a gleam. So was the cover of the notebook that lay open on his right knee.

A notebook? Brandi thought in disbelief. Why on earth was he taking notes? And why was he even *here*, without orders? The sooner she dealt with this mutinous employee the better.

Brandi slipped through the gate and went to the head of the line. "I need to talk to you," she murmured.

Zack ignored her. All his attention was focused on the child in his lap. The little girl was about four, and she was chattering merrily in what could have been a foreign language as far as Brandi was concerned; she could make out little resemblance to standard English. But though Zack's brow was furrowed a little as if he, too, found it difficult to understand the child, he was writing down a word now and then as she talked.

"Did you hear me?" Brandi muttered.

Zack's gaze lifted to study the line. "Certainly. I'll see you after I've finished with the kids."

Brandi had to bite her tongue to keep from firing him on the spot—but how would that look to the dozen children, and their parents, who were waiting in line?

She waited impatiently, trying not to tap her toes, as he eased the little girl off his lap, then beckoned the next child up and began to chat. At this rate, she thought, he'd be all afternoon getting through the remaining dozen kids. Which was no doubt exactly what he had in mind—stalling till Brandi got tired of waiting.

She shut the gate so the line wouldn't get any longer and put out the sign, kept handy for all the employees' breaks, which announced that Santa had gone to feed his reindeer but would return soon. Then she went back to stand beside the big chair. There was an infant on Zack's lap now, and his mother was backing off to get a photograph.

But finally the line was gone. Brandi waited till the last child was well out of earshot, and then turned on Zack. "What are you doing here?" she demanded.

"I don't see how it could be any more obvious."

"You were told you'd be called when we had an assignment for you!"

"And just when was that likely to be, Ms. Ogilvie? I don't think it would take much effort for you to find an excuse not to call me at all, so when I saw there was no Santa scheduled to work this afternoon, I volunteered."

"Don't you understand the store has a liability, Mr. Forrest? You can't just walk into this job without training."

"What's to learn? Your personnel director gave me a list of all the rules, and they're easy enough to memorize. Let's see—don't promise any toy unless the parent gives you a signal, just say *We'll see* instead. Never comment on a request for a little brother or sister. Just pretend you didn't hear it. Don't wear strong cologne or after-shave. Don't give candy without the parents' permission. Make a tour of Toyland every day before going on duty, in order to be familiar with the merchandise. Help the child to climb up, but don't lift— we're less likely to have scared little ones that way..." He paused. "And fewer injured Santas, too, no doubt, if they're not straining their backs lifting tots."

"That suggestion may have come from the corporate legal department," Brandi said stiffly. "But I don't see what that has to do with—"

"It certainly sounds like it."

She raised her voice. "The point is—"

"The point is that I have the rest of the hundred rules down pat, too—so why shouldn't I be working? Why should the kids be cheated of their opportunity to talk to Santa, just because it happens to be Monday afternoon?"

Brandi folded her arms and put her chin up. "There seems to be a basic disagreement about who's in charge here, Mr. —"

"Careful," Zack warned, and waved as a child stopped hopefully by the closed gate.

"*Claus*," Brandi said through clenched teeth. "Perhaps we should have this discussion somewhere other than Toyland."

Zack snapped his fingers. "I think you've finally hit on a good point, Ms. Ogilvie."

It was midafternoon, and the cafeteria should be practically empty. "How about talking it out over coffee?" Brandi suggested.

The child at the gate looked disappointed when Zack stood up. "When will you be back, Santa?" she called. "How long does it take to feed your reindeer?"

"Just a few minutes," Zack said. "I'll be back soon."

"If I were you, I wouldn't make any promises," Brandi muttered.

The lunch rush was long over, and only a few patrons were in the cafeteria, having a soft drink and resting their feet while they checked over their lists and purchases.

Zack poured two cups of coffee and carried them to an out-of-the-way table while Brandi gathered up cream, sugar, and napkins and told the counter attendant to put the charge on her bill.

"I suppose Santa never carries money," she said as she set her awkward load down on the table.

"Of course I do. But you asked for this date, and judging by how sensitive you were when I got your title wrong, you're probably the sort to take offense if I insist on paying. I'd be happy to hold your chair, though, unless that would irritate you, too.''

"Oh, sit down," she ordered.

But he held the chair for her anyway, before taking the seat across from her.

Brandi stirred sugar into her coffee and looked him over thoughtfully. "I feel as if I've walked into *Miracle on 34th Street*," she muttered.

Zack grinned.

The effect of his brilliant smile against the pure white beard and tanned face was stunning. He looked good in red, Brandi thought absently. The suit was a deep, rich ruby, and the color reflected nicely across his high cheekbones.

"If that's a polite way of asking if I think I'm the real Santa Claus, Brandi—no, I don't."

"Well, that's some relief. Wait a minute. How'd you know my name?"

Zack leaned forward confidingly. "Would you believe I used my X-ray vision to see through the file cabinets in the personnel director's office?''

"No.''

"That's good. We've established two things. I don't think I'm either Superman or Santa Claus, and you admit I'm not deluded about it. Now we're getting somewhere.''

"We're getting nowhere. I could fire you for this stunt, you know. You can't just go around putting yourself to work because you see a job you think needs doing.''

"I don't expect to be paid for this afternoon. It's sort of like giving out free samples—I volunteered in order to show you how well I can do the job. And you must admit I'm good at it.''

Brandi didn't want to admit anything of the sort, but she could hardly deny it, either. "That's beside the point, don't you think?"

"Hardly." Zack leaned back in his chair. "Tell the truth. Would you have called me?"

"Not directly. It's not my job. But I'd have made sure the personnel manager kept you in mind."

"What a comfort." His voice oozed sarcasm. "I might have got to work by Christmas Eve!"

"You have to remember you're low man when it comes to seniority. Knowing Ross doesn't make a difference where that's concerned, and it's only fair that the three Santas I hired before you will be considered first."

"There. You see? That's why I felt it necessary to make my own hours."

"Look, Mr. Forrest, I can't have employees setting their own schedules without considering what's best for the store."

"I *am* considering what's best for the store. You've now got a dozen kids who are happier with Tyler-Royale than they'd have been if I wasn't on duty this afternoon. And you'd have a dozen more if you'd left me at work instead of dragging me down here to drink coffee. So if you'll excuse me, I'll get back to my job." He pushed his chair back and stood up.

"Just because you know the CEO doesn't mean you can make the rules," Brandi warned.

He looked at her, gray eyebrows lifted in what looked like long-suffering patience.

Brandi reconsidered. He'd been flagrantly in the wrong to put himself to work like that. Still, she had to admit she couldn't exactly fire him over it; she'd have a little trouble explaining to Ross Clayton what was so terrible about his friend volunteering an afternoon to play Santa in order to prove himself.

And Zack Forrest looked as if he knew very well what she was thinking. He was standing beside the table with an air of disdain, clearly waiting for her to admit defeat.

Brandi capitulated. "You will not set your own hours anymore."

Zack set a booted foot on his chair and leaned over her. "How about if I promise to tell you before I go on duty?"

"That's not the same thing at all."

He smiled a little. "Well, I'm sure you'll work it all out. In the meantime, you know where to find me." He didn't pause till he reached the cafeteria door, and then only to politely hold it for a couple of elderly ladies.

There was no point in counting to ten in an effort to control her temper. Instead, Brandi counted the days till Christmas.

CHAPTER TWO

By the time Brandi left the store that night, it was almost closing time and the late-evening rush was beginning to die down. In the parking area of the enormous shopping mall, the cars were beginning to thin out. The air was cold and crisp; she knew she'd have been able to see the stars if it wasn't for the powerful banks of lights that held the winter darkness at bay. There would be no snow tonight.

A few miles away, in the big apartment complex where she lived, the windows of almost every unit glowed. In many of them, Christmas trees sparkled with light as tiny red and green and gold and white bulbs twinkled on and off. Almost every door displayed a wreath or a Santa or a Nativity scene.

And she could hear Christmas carols as she walked through the courtyard to her building. The sound of it made Brandi's head hurt. The music wasn't obnoxiously loud, but it was so darned distinctive, and so very inescapable. Christmas, she thought, had gotten out of hand.

Her own apartment, in contrast, was dim and quiet. She closed the door with a sigh of relief, turned on a couple of lamps, and put a classical CD on to play. Then she poured herself a glass of sherry and sat down on the couch to enjoy a little peace.

The room was something like a cocoon, cozy and comforting. The overstuffed furniture was covered in subdued colors and subtle patterns, nicely framed prints decorated the neutral-colored walls, and soft deep carpeting cushioned the floors. A room to be at ease in, it looked just as it did the other eleven months of the year— and that was one of the things Brandi liked best about it.

Here, there was no tree, no tinsel, no mistletoe. She didn't have to deal with the sights and smells of the holiday. She didn't have to listen to perpetual Christmas carols. In fact, when she was safely snuggled into her own living room, she could pretend it wasn't Christmas at all.

And considering the day she'd had, that was a blessing.

She let her head rest against the soft back of the couch and closed her eyes. How on earth was she going to handle her new Santa?

In the two years she'd managed the Oak Park store, she'd never had an employee like him, that was sure. She'd never even *heard* of an employee who set his own hours in defiance of the store's schedule, who contradicted the boss, who acted as if he knew her job better than she did.

But then, she'd never hired a friend of the boss before, either. She'd like to call up Ross Clayton and ask what kind of blackmail material Zack had on him; it must be something extraordinary to account for the kind of special treatment the man seemed to expect. For the life of her, she couldn't think of anything that infamous.

She finished her sherry and wandered into the kitchen to dig through the freezer for something that would be easy to cook. There wasn't much variety left; she'd have to fit in time to stop at the supermarket in the next few days. Certainly she'd have to go before the weekend, when things would really get hectic again.

The phone rang. She made a face and thought about ignoring it, then sighed and picked it up anyway. There might be a security problem at the store.

Casey Amos said, "I saw you with Santa in the cafeteria this afternoon. What's going on, Brandi?"

"We were having a chat. Why?"

"You should hear what the grapevine's saying."

"Casey, I stopped being interested in store gossip a long time ago."

"All right, then, I won't tell you," Casey said cheerfully. "It's a good story, though. And I could see the sparks you were striking off each other."

"The only sparks you saw were pure irritation."

"Ah. Then it is true Ross made you hire him?"

Brandi kept her voice level. "I wonder who started that rumor."

"You just did—telling me you were irritated. If hiring him had been your idea, and he annoyed you so much, he'd have been out the door in two minutes flat."

Brandi wanted to bite her tongue off. Just yesterday she'd have had the sense to think it over before she spoke, and she'd have refused Casey's bait. Zack Forrest had struck once more. At this rate, by Christmas she wouldn't have a shred of judgment left.

"Instead," Casey went on, "he finished his shift and went home. In fact, since I was clocking out at the same time, he walked me to my car."

"Congratulations."

"He seems perfectly nice—but I didn't feel the same kind of sparks you were giving off this afternoon, so don't worry."

"Why do I put up with you, Casey?"

"Because I'm the best department head you've got, and when I get a store of my own next year you're going to cry over losing me."

"True. Still—"

"And because I'm so discreet. I won't pass along a word of what you've confided in me tonight."

"I wasn't aware I'd bared my soul," Brandi said acidly. "If that's why you called, I appreciate the thought, but—"

Casey's voice took on a more serious note. "No, actually I'm checking on the menu for the Christmas party. It's only two weeks off, you know, so I have to get an order to the caterer right away."

"Casey, you know I don't care what you serve at the Christmas party."

"We can do it for the same money as last year if we leave out the shrimp."

"Didn't you say the staff loved the shrimp last year?"

"Yes. Still, everything else has gone so high, and you did say we had to stick to the budget...."

"Have the shrimp. I'll make up the shortfall personally. Just don't tell anybody, all right?"

"And ruin your reputation as the biggest Scrooge in the chain? I wouldn't dream of it. Are you going to put your name in the gift-exchange drawing this year?"

"Of course not. Why do you think I insisted you make participation voluntary?"

"Still, you seem to be softening a little. Maybe it's Santa's influence. You seem inspired, somehow."

Brandi gritted her teeth. "The only thing my new Santa has inspired in me is fury."

"I wasn't referring to any person in particular," Casey murmured. "I was talking about the spirit of Christmas. But *you* assumed I meant your new Santa. How interesting that you thought of him right off!"

There were times when the cramped size of Brandi's office had its advantages; she'd found that meetings and conferences tended to move along very promptly when the participants found themselves sitting on bookcases and file cabinets.

Her usual Tuesday morning meeting with all the store's department heads was winding down, just a few minutes before the business day began, when Dora came into her office with a slip of paper and slid it across the desk without a word.

Brandi unfolded the note, still half-listening to the report from the head of the electronics department. "Mrs. Townsend of the Kansas City store wants you to call her," Dora had written in her cramped, neat hand.

That's odd, Brandi thought. If the matter had been crucial, Dora would have summoned her from the meeting. Since it wasn't, why hadn't the secretary just held the message till after the meeting broke up?

Then Brandi realized she'd overlooked the second part of the note. "And your Santa popped in just now to tell you he's going to work this morning," Dora had written.

Brandi sighed. Did everybody in the store now think of Zack Forrest as her very own private Santa?

She dismissed the department heads and followed them out to the alcove. "Dora, did Mrs. Townsend tell you what she wanted?"

"No. She just said to call her when it's convenient, that she'd be in the store all day." Dora warily eyed the slip of paper in Brandi's hand. "I didn't know what to do about your Santa."

"Neither does anyone else," Brandi admitted.

"I'm not even sure what he was talking about. I asked him why he didn't just punch the time clock like the rest of the employees instead of reporting to you, and he said you were expecting him. So I thought I should tell you right away."

I wish you hadn't, Brandi thought. If she didn't know Zack was down there in the big chair in front of Santa's Workshop, stirring up trouble, she could simply go about her business. Now that she knew, she'd have to do something about it—she couldn't simply pretend to be oblivious. No manager could let a brand-new employee go around creating his own schedule and making a fool of her. If that word got out, Brandi Ogilvie would be a laughingstock throughout the whole chain.

But she'd spent the night thinking about it, and she still couldn't quite imagine how she was going to stop Zack Forrest from doing precisely what he pleased.

She could refuse to pay him, of course, but she didn't think that would stand up long once he had another chat with Ross Clayton. After all, he was doing the work for which he'd been hired—and she didn't think the fact that he wasn't precisely up to Brandi's specifications would carry any more weight with Ross than it had yesterday when she'd tried to get out of hiring him in the first place.

Well, if she couldn't get rid of him, she'd better give him some regular hours. At least then she'd look as if she was still in control. "Dora, will you find out when the next real Santa's due to come in?"

"Certainly." Dora looked a bit puzzled.

"Better yet, go over to the employees' lounge and make a copy of the schedule for the next week, and bring it into my office. Oh, and Dora—try not to let anybody see what you're doing."

Dora looked even more confused. Brandi just smiled and went back to her office.

She dismissed Zack from her mind for the moment and settled back at her desk to call Whitney Townsend in Kansas City. She always enjoyed talking to Whitney; the woman might have anything in mind, from a personnel swap to a practical joke on the CEO. And since she was not only a senior manager but a vice president of the Tyler-Royale chain, she could get by with either—or almost anything in between.

Brandi's call was passed to Whitney's office with machine-gun efficiency. "How are you?" Whitney demanded as soon as she picked up the phone. "I haven't heard from you in weeks."

"You know how things get this time of year."

"Exactly. That's why I expected a call before the Christmas season kicked into high gear. Don't you know you're supposed to phone your mentor once a month at least?" The smile in her voice took any sting out of the words.

"I've tried," Brandi said crisply. "But I didn't bother to leave a message last time I called, because you were in San Antonio sorting out the problems in the store there."

"Oh, that. Ross seems to be short a troubleshooter at the moment, so I got roped in to handle things."

"I assumed that's what happened. At any rate, I thought you probably had enough to deal with. The time before that you were vacationing in Hawaii when I called. Your secretary offered me the number, but I know better than to disturb you on a second honeymoon."

Whitney laughed. "Good thinking. No problems, then?"

Brandi thought about Zack Forrest, and sighed. She couldn't even begin to put that particular difficulty into words. "Nothing more than usual."

"Well, that's good. Nevertheless, I want to check for myself, so I'm coming up to see you at the end of the week. Hold Saturday evening open for me, all right?"

Brandi flipped the page in her desk calendar to write the appointment down. "You don't mean the night of the corporate Christmas party," she said slowly.

"That's exactly what I mean. And don't you dare miss it."

"Whitney, you know I hate those things."

"Yes, and I also know that every year you come up with another spectacular reason for not coming. In fact, Ross suggested I not call you, because he wanted to see what you'd use to get out of it this time. You're running so late at sending your regrets that he figures it'll have to be a doozy of an excuse."

"But of course you didn't obey his wishes."

"Well, it wasn't quite a direct order," Whitney said reasonably. "So I just ignored him."

Brandi wished she'd dared to ignore Ross on the question of Zack Forrest. Someday, she thought dreamily, she'd be a corporate vice president and she could. Not that it made any difference right now. "Can't we just have lunch instead, Whitney? We won't really be able to talk at the party, you know."

Dora opened the door and quietly laid the Santa schedule on Brandi's desk.

Whitney said firmly, "I'm flying up on Saturday afternoon and back on Sunday, so it's the party or nothing. I have a store to manage myself, you know."

Brandi capitulated. "Then I'll be at the party to see you. But I hope you don't insist on my having a good time otherwise."

Whitney only laughed, and Brandi put down the phone and picked up the Santa schedule. Dora hadn't stopped with the week's calendar; she'd brought the whole month's, all the way through Christmas Eve.

Brandi had worked like fury on that schedule. It was the perfectly arranged product of two seasons' worth of observation of the store's mix of customers. Any time there was likely to be a large number of children in the store—late afternoons, evenings and weekends, mostly—there would be a Santa on duty. And the hours were perfectly divided between the three elderly, white-haired, bearded men Brandi had hired to play the part.

Now, in order to leave room for Zack Forrest, she was going to have to throw it all out and start over.

She wanted to growl. No, what she really wanted to do was go down to Toyland and give one irrepressible Santa a black eye. But that was guaranteed to make things worse.

She got out a fresh schedule sheet and began to draw boxes.

Keeping things as fair as possible, while trying not to cheat any of the men she'd hired first, would be a challenge. In fact, just the idea of calling her handpicked Santas in and explaining the changes gave her heartburn. They weren't going to be happy at having their calendars rearranged for no reason, and she didn't blame them. But she could hardly come straight out and tell them they'd been displaced by an upstart who happened to know the boss.

Unless... Maybe there was another way.

She turned the original schedule this way and that, then smiled, reached for a red marker, and drew a series of neat lines. Then she tucked the page in the pocket of her suit jacket and left her office. "Dora, I'll be in Toyland talking to Santa."

"Good luck," Dora muttered. "I don't envy you the job."

The line outside Santa's Workshop was moving along faster this morning then it had yesterday; most of the children were very small, and the parents seemed more interested in photographs than in conversations. Brandi closed the gate, put the "Santa's Feeding His Reindeer" sign in place, and strolled to the head of the line to stand near the big chair.

Zack had seen her coming the moment she'd gotten off the escalator, Brandi was sure of that, though he didn't look up. In fact, an observer would swear Santa hadn't taken his attention from the child on his lap. But Brandi knew he was aware of her presence, because she could feel a sudden pulse of energy coming from him— as if he'd been waiting impatiently for her and was relieved that she'd finally appeared.

She stood beside the big chair, just inside his peripheral vision, and folded her arms, trying to look as if she could comfortably stay there forever. She knew better than to suggest Zack leave even a single child waiting, but perhaps if she just stood there silently, he'd get nervous and hurry things along.

A couple of minutes later he looked up at her with a quick smile and a quizzical quirk to his fake-gray eyebrows. "Are you certain the reindeer need feeding *again*, Ms. Ogilvie?"

Brandi kept her voice level with an effort. "I'm afraid they do, Santa."

"And you came all the way down to help me. How thoughtful of you!"

The year-old child on Zack's lap gurgled, and her mother picked her up. "Nice touch. I hope you both enjoy yourselves on your break." She winked at Brandi. "Bet I can guess what you'd like for Christmas from this particular Santa."

Brandi felt color rising in her face as she remembered what Casey had said about the sparks she'd seen passing between Brandi and Zack yesterday. The conclusion Casey had jumped to was an idiotic one, of course— and this young mother was being just as silly to think that the electricity she saw must have a romantic element to it.

But Brandi had to bite her lip hard to subdue the blush. She didn't look at Zack, but she could sense he was smiling, obviously enjoying her discomfort.

The next child had been listening to the exchange. He marched up to Zack, folded his arms, and announced, "Santa's just for kids. My mom says so. Big people aren't supposed to ask you to bring them things."

Zack's eyebrows soared. "Why on earth shouldn't they? Big people have dreams, too." He looked up at Brandi appraisingly. "What *would* you like for Christmas, Ms. Ogilvie?"

"For New Year's Day to come three weeks early," Brandi said.

Zack choked, and it was almost half a minute before he recovered enough to take the child on his knee and get back to business. With her equilibrium restored, Brandi settled back to wait for him to deal with the rest of the line. At least, she thought, he wasn't likely to ask her any more leading questions in public!

He was better than she'd expected at the job, she had to admit. He'd done his homework, or else he was a phenomenal actor, for not a toy was mentioned that Zack didn't seem to recognize. And he didn't simply acknowledge the requests, either; he engaged each child in conversation about his wishes, and asked how he'd decided on that special item.

Brandi shifted impatiently from one foot to the other. "That's charming, Santa, but—"

Zack's eyes widened. "You mean you actually think I'm doing something right for a change?"

"Yes and no. I don't see the point of asking them why they've chosen a particular toy."

"I'm trying to make certain they really want it, and haven't simply been swayed by television ads or what their friends say."

A mother waiting in line nodded in approval. "Last year my son got everything on his list and didn't play with any of it. I was pretty annoyed, I'll tell you, when all those expensive toys turned out to be just a fad. I appreciate your taking time to make sure, Santa Claus.''

Zack shot Brandi a look that said, *See? Maybe I do know what I'm doing*.

She said, under her breath, ''I still think it's more likely you're trying to delay till I get tired of standing here.''

''You?'' he murmured. ''I'm beginning to think you're inexhaustible, Ms. Ogilvie.'' But eventually the kids were all satisfied, and Brandi and Zack were alone outside Santa's Workshop. Zack stood up, stretched, and tucked his leather-covered notebook into a capacious pocket. ''I must say it's nice to have a break. That chair isn't as comfortable as it looks. Coffee? It's my turn to buy, I believe.''

The same counter attendant was working in the cafeteria. ''Two days in a row?'' she murmured. ''This is getting to be a habit, Ms. Ogilvie.''

Oh, that's just great, Brandi thought. If Casey was right, the store's grapevine was already working overtime. By the end of the day, her two cups of coffee with Santa would probably have grown into a full-fledged affair. And if the tale escaped the Oak Park store and made the rounds of the chain, gossip would probably have her moving to the North Pole to live with him.

Zack stirred sugar into his coffee and looked thoughtfully across the table at her. ''So what do you really want for Christmas, Brandi?''

She decided to ignore the name; complaining, she suspected, would only encourage him. ''You're off duty now. Remember?''

He didn't seem to hear. ''Emeralds? They'd look good against that auburn hair and fair skin of yours.''

''I hardly think Santa's likely to bring me emeralds.''

''Well, that's true—at least this Santa. We hardly know each other, so it wouldn't be at all proper for me to give you jewelry.'' His gaze dropped to the cluster of diamonds on her left hand. ''To say nothing of the fact that Mr. Ogilvie would probably object. Tell me, *is* there a Mr. Ogilvie?''

This, Brandi thought, is getting out of hand. ''I can't think why you'd need to know.''

''Can't you? Well, never mind for now. Surely there's something you'd like for Christmas. Something simple, maybe, like peace on earth...'' Zack snapped his fingers. ''I know! How about a white Christmas?''

''That would be too late to do us any good,'' Brandi said crisply. ''On the other hand, a nice half-inch snowfall sometime this week would put every shopper in the holiday spirit and raise the season's sales by at least ten percent.''

Zack shook his head sadly.

''Only half an inch, though.'' Brandi sipped her coffee. ''Much more than that jams up traffic and people stay home.''

''You have a very unromantic view of the holiday.''

''So would you, I expect, if you'd been working Christmas retail for a decade.''

Zack looked startled. ''Ten years? You're not old enough.''

''Yes, I am. I started working part-time for Tyler-Royale when I was in high school, right in the middle of the Christmas season. But I didn't come down here to talk about me. I've got your work assignments for the rest of the month.''

Zack pulled out his notebook and flipped it open.

''That reminds me,'' Brandi said. ''Don't you think you ought to ditch the notebook?''

''Why?'' He didn't sound argumentative, just curious.

"Surely I shouldn't have to explain to you that Santa remembers everything a child says and does. It's part of the mystique."

Zack frowned. "You mean you haven't ever heard of the old guy making a list and checking it twice? I take back what I said earlier, Brandi. You're not unromantic about Christmas, you're downright oblivious."

Something about his tone annoyed Brandi; he didn't need to treat her like Scrooge, for heaven's sake. "I must say I don't see what good it does to write down what a child wants. It's not like you're seriously going to hunt up these kids on Christmas Eve and deliver toys." She wrinkled her brow. "Are you?"

"Of course not."

"Right. How could you, when you haven't the foggiest idea who the child is or where he lives? That proves my point, you know. Writing all this stuff down takes up time and paper for nothing." She reached for his notebook, and knocked loose the white carnation pinned to the lapel of her forest green suit.

Zack slid the notebook out from under her hand and tucked it back in his pocket. "On the contrary," he said soberly. "Taking notes make the kids feel that I'm listening to them very seriously. They're reassured to know their requests are written down safely in Santa's book. So, while I thank you for your concern, I believe I'll keep on just as I've been doing."

Brandi glared at him for an instant, then turned her attention to her carnation. It was useless to argue with him, she thought. She was obviously not going to convince him she was right, and the issue simply wasn't important enough to issue a direct order. That was why she'd asked a question in the first place, instead of just telling him to leave his notebook at home; Brandi had learned long ago to choose her battlefields more carefully than that.

Zack reached across the table. For an instant, his fingers almost encircled her wrist as he pulled her hand away from the carnation. Then he straightened the flower himself, setting the pin firmly into the wool of her lapel.

Brandi thought she could feel the warmth of his fingertips against her collarbone. The sensation was strictly imaginary, of course, she reminded herself, since not only the suit but a silky blouse lay between his hand and her bare skin. Still, the contact seemed to burn all the way to her bones.

"You said something about my work hours?" Zack reminded her.

Brandi pulled the Santa schedule out of her pocket and slid it across the table. "The blocks I've marked in red are yours."

Would he argue? she wondered. Or threaten? Would he get angry, or try to negotiate?

Zack studied the page, and then his gaze lifted to meet hers. At this distance, his eyes looked even darker than usual against the spun white floss of his beard. "You've marked all the times you hadn't already scheduled a Santa."

"Yes," Brandi admitted. "Since you seem to have adopted a good number of those hours anyway, I thought you might as well have every last one of them."

"It's generous of you, but—"

Brandi smiled. "Isn't it?" she said easily. "I *have* given you more time than any of the other Santas will work, so I hope you won't make an issue of it. They might feel left out."

"Considering the way these hours are spread around, I doubt they'll be jealous." Zack glanced at the paper again. "Two hours in the morning, one at closing time, a half hour through the supper break...this ought to keep me busy.''

''If you don't like the schedule, Zack...''

''Oh, I absolutely adore it. I can get all my Christmas shopping done while I'm between shifts.''

Brandi started to feel just a bit uneasy. The schedule she'd given him was nasty—the man wouldn't have an entire half day to call his own for the next month, but his work was so split up that all of his hours didn't add up to a full-time paycheck, either. Shouldn't he have at least tried to change her mind, to talk her into giving him some more reasonable hours? She studied him covertly. She couldn't detect a hint of strain in Zack's smile, and that worried her.

''Of course, I may have to pitch a tent in the parking lot to be sure I'm not late for any of my numerous curtain times,'' he said, ''but as long as you don't mind that little nuisance—''

Brandi relaxed a little. There was an edge to his voice, so slight that if she hadn't been listening intently, she'd have missed it. So he wasn't as sanguine as he'd pretended. Now he'd no doubt start to negotiate.

Well, that was all right with Brandi; she was perfectly willing to compromise. At least this time she'd be dealing from a position of strength, unlike the matter of his notebook. Brandi thought it made a nice change, everything considered.

''That's why I gave you your schedule for the whole month,'' she said agreeably. ''So you could plan ahead.''

''I'll do that. Now, since I'm supposed to be working at the moment, I'd better get back to it or you'll probably fire me for not showing up for my assigned times.''

He folded the schedule, tucked it into an inner pocket, and left the cafeteria without a backward glance.

Guilt washed over Brandi like a wave across the deck of a sailboat. The schedule she'd given him was worse than nasty, she admitted; it was unconscionable. She'd never before assigned an employee to that kind of random, scattered hours over such a long period of time, and she wouldn't stand for any of her department heads doing so, either. It wasn't fair to expect someone to be always on call and ready for work for a full month, without a single break.

Only store managers have to do that, she thought with a tinge of wry humor.

But why hadn't Zack made a fuss? Why hadn't he tried to get a change? Was he intending to go straight to Ross to complain?

She didn't think so. From what she'd seen of him so far, he wasn't the sort to hide his feelings or ask someone else to fight his battles. He hadn't hesitated to stand up for his convictions about the darned notebook so why would he have shrunk from arguing about his working hours?

Maybe he was simply further down on his luck than she'd thought. Maybe he really needed the work.

Brandi swallowed hard and tried to remember what the schedule had looked like. It wasn't too bad for the next couple of days, she thought. Not till the weekend did the scattered, fragmented hours really start. She'd see how it worked out for a day or two, and then...

Well, if she had to go to him and back down, it wouldn't be the first time Brandi Ogilvie had admitted to making a mistake.

She just didn't relish the thought of facing Zack with an apology.

CHAPTER THREE

BRANDI leaned on the fence that surrounded Santa's Workshop and watched admiringly as the white-haired man sitting in the big chair encouraged the child in his lap to tug on his long white beard. The child gave it a healthy yank, and Santa yelped in what Brandi thought was only slightly exaggerated discomfort.

The child's eyes widened. "Mommy, it's *real*," he said. "This must be the *real* Santa!"

Now that, Brandi thought, was more like it. Too bad Zack wasn't here to see a qualified professional at work.

Not that she was exactly anxious for him to show up. She hadn't seen Zack in nearly thirty-six hours, since he'd stalked out of the cafeteria yesterday morning. She suspected he was taking care to stay out of her way.

In fact, Brandi wouldn't have been a bit surprised if he hadn't shown up for work today at all, but instead had gone back to see his friend, Ross Clayton. She'd even wasted a little time considering what Ross might have to say about how she'd handled this entire affair, and she'd had to remind herself that her boss was generally a reasonable sort.

Still, she'd ended up sending Dora to the employees' lounge to check the time clock, and only when the secretary came back to report that Zack had indeed clocked in to work his assigned morning shift had Brandi really relaxed. Then she'd devoted herself to the paperwork that had been building up on her desk for the last week. She'd spent the whole morning and much of the afternoon in her office, and it was only as the early winter darkness was closing in that she finally pushed her papers aside and went to make her regular tour of the store.

She watched as Santa tipped his face down to look at a child over the top of his half glasses. The glasses were a perfect finishing touch, and the lenses were real—she'd made it a point to notice in the man's employment interview.

"Now that's a switch," a low, rich voice said beside her. "The admiring look on your face, I mean."

She wheeled around to face Zack. "What are you doing here?" She could have bitten off the tip of her tongue the second the words were out; why should it be any particular concern of hers if he wanted to hang around Santa's Workshop and observe?

The corner of Zack's mouth quirked, but there was little humor in the expression. "I'm just coming off duty, after a half hour in the chair while this guy had his dinner. Since it was your idea, I expected you'd at least remember."

Brandi had forgotten. Why hadn't she been smart enough to keep a copy of that ridiculous schedule she'd given him? Because it was so very ridiculous, she reminded herself, that she hadn't foreseen any possibility it would ever go into effect—that was why.

Zack must have just come from the small dressing room concealed within the shell of Santa's Workshop, for he was wearing street clothes. Brandi had gotten so used to seeing him in the red velvet suit and the white beard that she was startled by his gray trousers and matching cashmere sweater, and more so by his chiseled profile. He looked tired, and there was no hint of a dimple.

Brandi found herself wondering about that dimple. Had it been to the left of his mouth, or the right? She couldn't quite remember. Not that it mattered, of course;

she didn't care if she ever saw it again. And it was no concern of hers whether Zack Forrest smiled or not.

"He's good," Zack said. He nodded toward the Santa.

Brandi was surprised that he'd volunteered so much. "Of course he is. That's why I hired him."

"Careful—you don't want the kids to hear that."

She was annoyed with herself for the slip. "Thanks for the reminder," she said sweetly. "I'll be more careful now, so don't feel you have to stick around to keep me in check."

Zack didn't seem to notice the saccharine tone. "Where do you think I'd be going?"

"You surely don't expect me to believe you've actually pitched a tent in the parking lot. I assumed you were on your way home. If you've finished work—"

"But I haven't. I'm off for two hours, then I have another hour on duty just before the store closes."

"But I thought, since you weren't in uniform..."

"I assumed you wouldn't like the idea of an extra Santa wandering around the store."

"No, I wouldn't."

"And since I have a tendency to get claustrophobic, I don't relish the thought of sitting in the dressing room. It's pretty tiny, you know. So that means changing my clothes every time I come off duty."

Brandi bit her lip and debated how to confess that she really hadn't intended it to work out that way.

But before she could find the words, Zack added, "I must admit my Christmas shopping is coming along well, though. I've been killing time by looking over the merchandise, and I've almost taken care of my whole list. What about you? Are you off duty now?"

"No—I'm just making my regular rounds. I try to walk through every department in the store at least twice a day."

One of Zack's dark eyebrows lifted quizzically. "Is this your first trip, or have you been avoiding Toyland today?"

"I haven't been avoiding anything. It's a critical time of year, and I've been very busy in my office." Brandi didn't owe him any explanations, of course, but the question made her feel a little uneasy. *Was* that one of the reasons she'd kept herself so fully occupied all day?

"I'm glad you explained," Zack said earnestly. "You see, I thought it might have something to do with not wanting to run into me."

Brandi's uneasiness flared into full-fledged annoyance. Zack had no cause to indulge in that sort of speculation, and she'd better put a stop to it right away. But keep it light, she warned herself. "Why on earth wouldn't I want to see you?"

Zack started to smile. "You do, then? Well, that's reassuring. It makes my life worthwhile, to know that you've been looking forward to seeing me again after all."

Brandi winced. She'd walked right into that one.

Zack was merciless. "In fact, since we're both planning to stroll through the store right now, we can do it together. Won't that be fun? Which direction are you heading?"

Whichever way she indicated, he'd no doubt adapt his plans to trail along just to annoy her. Not that he wasn't already doing a good job of that—if there was a contest for irritating the boss, he could be named employee of the month.

"I'm not planning to stroll, exactly," she said. "I'm in a hurry, so—"

"Are you anxious to get done and go home after all?"

"Not particularly. I'll be here till closing time—I usually am this time of year. But I have other things to do. So, since I'd hate to rush you and keep you from looking around to your heart's content—''

Zack leaned against a pillar and folded his arms across his chest. ''I suppose your Christmas shopping is all done?'' he challenged.

''That's right.''

''You don't even need to look for one little thing to finish out your list?'' He whistled admiringly. ''You know, I'd convinced myself that someone who's got such a case of glooms about the holiday would put off shopping till the last possible moment. But you are a wonder of efficiency, Brandi.''

''Well, I'm glad the question entertained you, but—''

''I wonder how I could have been so wrong about you. Unless . . . Yes, I've got it. I'll bet you're giving everyone on your list Tyler-Royale gift certificates.''

He was dead right, as a matter of fact, and that made Brandi nervous. How had he guessed that? ''So what if I am? There's nothing wrong with gift certificates.''

''I suppose not,'' Zack said. He didn't sound as if he believed it. ''One easy stop at the customer service desk and you're done. Everybody gets what they want, Tyler-Royale rings up the sales, and you've even cut back on after-Christmas returns and exchanges. What a perfectly thoughtful solution for everybody!''

''You don't need to make it sound like a breach of good manners.'' Brandi stepped away from the fence. ''It's been nice talking to you, Zack, but since we're not going the same direction . . .'' She started walking down the broad aisle toward housewares.

Zack fell into step beside her. ''Why *are* you so anti-Christmas? I'd really like to know. If you hate the pressure of retail sales at this time of year, there are other jobs, you know.''

"I hope I won't always be at this level, so that I won't always have to deal with Christmas panic. But in the meantime, I live for my job the other eleven months of the year, and I've learned to simply endure Christmas. It equals out."

"The job is what you live for?" There was an incredulous note in his voice.

"What's so amazing? I have other interests, you know, but this season of the year there's no time for them. The job has to come first. Or don't you think any woman should be more interested in a mere job than in other things?" Brandi's voice was tart.

"I wouldn't dare tell all women what to do. I just meant, if that's the case, there's obviously no Mr. Ogilvie after all."

It wasn't a question, and yet, since it was pointless to evade such a direct statement, Brandi answered. "No, there isn't."

"Has there ever been?"

She stopped beside a towering stack of small appliances—mixers, toasters, blenders. "I beg your pardon?"

"I just asked—"

"I know what you asked. My personal history is none of your affair."

Zack shrugged. "All right. Whatever you say." He picked up a box. "Do you think my sister would like a vegetable steamer?"

"Since I don't know your sister, I haven't the foggiest." Brandi's voice was curt.

Zack didn't seem to take offense. "I've already bought her one, you see, but now that I think it over, it just doesn't seem right." His eyes lighted up. "Or maybe I'll just give it to you—you're the sort to appreciate a really practical gift. Well, I'll have plenty of time to think about it before I decide. I've still got more than an hour to kill before I have to go back to work."

That reminded Brandi of the damned schedule. The only thing she really remembered about it was that as the days went on the hours got worse. That meant this had been one of the milder days, even though the work shifts he'd described had sounded bad enough to send most employees into fits. She was going to have to back down, and the sooner she did so, the less painful it would be.

She took a deep breath. "Look, Zack... if you want to simplify that schedule I gave you, it's fine with me. We don't really need a Santa during the dinner break, and it's a nuisance for you to sit around and wait in order to do half an hour's work."

He didn't nod, or smile, or frown. He didn't do anything at all.

His lack of reaction puzzled Brandi. "Or for the last hour we're open, either," she went on hurriedly. "We don't need to offer a Santa then."

Zack still gave no indication that he'd even heard her, but she knew he must have.

She tried to make a joke of it. "All good little kids are home in bed by that time anyway. So if you'd like to call it a day right now—"

"You're cutting my hours?"

"I'm trying to give you a break!"

Zack shook his head slightly, as if he was disappointed in her. Or perhaps he simply couldn't believe his ears. "Oh, no, Brandi. I wouldn't dream of asking for special treatment. You assigned me certain blocks of time to work, and I'm not complaining."

Brandi blinked in astonishment. "All right," she snapped. "If that's the way you want it, go right ahead."

Zack smiled, and his dimple flashed for just an instant. "After all, you're not asking me for anything so out of the ordinary. I'm sure you'll be here every single hour that I am. Won't you?"

The dimple was in his left cheek. Brandi wanted to growl at herself for noticing.

She could feel the change of pace in the store as closing time approached. Even though she was still in her office, out of sight of the sales floors, she could almost hear the beeping of cash registers being cleared, of computers humming to a halt, of lights clicking off.

Brandi signed the last of a stack of letters and put them aside for Dora to mail in the morning. Then she took off her white carnation—a bit bedraggled now, after twelve hours pinned to her lapel—and dropped it into the wastebasket beside her desk.

The rest of the executive offices were dark, though in the employees' lounge next door several workers were putting on coats and boots for the journey home.

The store itself was never really dark; light was the best security measure. But the sales floors looked different with the banks of brilliant display lighting shut off. And the store sounded different, too. For one thing, the Christmas music, which was so cheerfully relentless all day, had at last died into blessed silence.

The escalators had already been shut off. Brandi walked down slowly, running a practiced eye over the entire floor. Outside Toyland, she spotted a red suit; Zack was leaning on the fence by Santa's Worship, talking to a group of kids. And what they were still doing in the store after closing time was anyone's guess. The kids were what had drawn her attention, she told herself. She certainly hadn't been looking for Zack.

A uniformed security guard called her name, and Brandi met him in electronics, where he was checking the display cases to be sure they were locked. The Doberman by his side perked his ears and looked her over with interest. Brandi kept a respectful distance; the dog was securely leashed, but it would take only a nudge to his harness and a word from the guard to turn him into a vicious machine.

"The head of mall security warned me they had a strange-looking guy hanging around the parking lot earlier tonight," the guard said. "They're suggesting all employees leave by the main entrances. Santa said he'd walk you to your car."

"That's not necessary. Be sure you tell everybody."

He nodded. "I posted a sign on the employee exit."

Zack had shooed the kids toward the entrance, but he was still leaning on the fence, watching as Brandi approached. "Ready to go?" he said.

"You needn't bother, Zack."

"Don't flatter yourself. It's no bother at all, because I'm going that way myself."

"How gracious of you," Brandi murmured. "Still, you must want to change clothes before you go."

"Again? No, thanks. When I take off the suit this time, I'm getting straight into a hot shower."

Why that comment should make her face grow warm was beyond Brandi's understanding. It was a perfectly straightforward statement, nothing more. "Well, don't let me keep you from it."

"The only thing that's slowing me down is the fact that we're standing here talking," he pointed out.

That was true enough, so Brandi started for the entrance. But she murmured, "Can't you take a hint?"

"Of course I can. That wasn't exactly a hint you issued, that was a sledgehammer."

The metal-mesh gate was already closed, except for a gap just wide enough for her to slip through. "I can get myself across the parking lot to my car, you know. We have these little episodes from time to time, and it never amounts to anything."

"But if you don't get to your car, and they find your body tomorrow..."

"You think the authorities will suspect you?"

"Of course they won't," he said promptly. "There must be dozens of people who'll fall under suspicion first. I just hate to think who Ross would replace you with."

"Thanks for keeping my ego cut down to size."

"You're quite welcome."

The grand concourse of the mall was quiet; the usual hurly-burly was reduced to the click of heels here and there and the quiet splash of the fountain. They crossed to the main door, and Zack held it open. Snowflakes swirled in on a blast of air, which sent chills up Brandi's spine.

Sealed in the artificial cocoon of the building all day, Brandi hadn't given a thought to the weather. "I didn't even know it was snowing. What a nuisance."

Zack bowed deeply. "My pleasure, madam. Half an inch of snow, delivered sometime this week, I believe you said?"

Brandi glared at him. "If you think you're getting credit for this because a couple of days ago I happened to say a little snow would help sales... Don't you have a coat?"

"I left it in my car."

"Not one of your brighter moves, I'd say."

"Oh, this suit's surprisingly warm. That's one of the things I've been meaning to talk to you about, by the way. Do you suppose we could turn down the heat around Santa's Workshop? Or the lights, at least? It's a little steamy."

Brandi shrugged. "Maybe if you weren't wearing so much fur..."

Zack brushed a few snowflakes off his white-fur lapel. "You mean this? It's fake. Kids might be allergic to the real stuff."

"I should have known."

"Besides, I'm not the only one who's uncomfortable with the temperatures up there."

"Oh? Have you polled the other Santas? I suppose next you'll try to organize them into a union and picket if you don't get what you want."

"Not a bad idea. I'll have to start making my list of demands. Where's your car?"

Brandi waved a hand toward the farthest row of the parking lot. "Sorry it's so far, but it was your idea to come out here."

"I'm not complaining."

But he must be cold, Brandi thought. Snow had already frosted his velvet cap, and a few flakes had caught in his eyelashes. She hadn't realized before how long and dark they were. She really ought to send him back to the mall, or directly to his car, instead of letting him walk on with her and get colder.

Right. She'd probably have just as much success at that as with anything else she'd tried to make him stop doing.

"I wasn't just talking about the Santas anyway," Zack went on. "The kids are uncomfortable, too. Most of them have their coats on, you know. In fact, a cooler temperature in the whole store might be more popular with shoppers."

"Why don't you start asking them? You can put that notebook to some good use for a change. Just write me a report in a couple of weeks and I'll take it under consideration."

But Zack didn't seem to hear.

Brandi followed his gaze. Twenty yards away, a woman and a small child were walking hand in hand toward a parked car. At least, the woman was walking; the child—perhaps six or seven years old—was hanging back, staring at Zack and saying two words over and over. "Santa Claus... Santa Claus!"

The woman frowned a little and shook her head. "Peggy, no. I told you we only came to look at the Christmas lights."

"But if I can just talk to Santa Claus—"

"What would you like to tell me?" Zack called.

"Zack," Brandi said under her breath. "Isn't this covered in the rules? The mother doesn't want you. And a Tyler-Royale Santa doesn't go marching up to kids. He waits to be approached."

"I'm not working for you at the moment, Brandi. Remember?"

Before she could protest, he was gone. His long stride ate up the distance despite the slick snow underfoot, and before Brandi could catch up he'd crouched down beside the child. "Are you going to come sit on Santa's lap tomorrow and tell me what you'd like for Christmas?"

"No," the child said. It was hardly more than a whisper.

"Why not?" Zack asked gently. "Surely you're not scared of me. I'm nothing to be scared of."

The woman said, "You can't give my daughter what she wants for Christmas, sir."

There was a note of pain in her voice—and a veneer of dignity—that made Brandi look more carefully at the pair. The child's winter coat was obviously not new and was much too big for her. The woman's was rather threadbare, and neither of them was wearing boots. But there was a pink ribbon carefully tied in the child's hair, and the mother's back was very straight.

Zack didn't move; he was still at the child's eye level as he glanced up at her mother. His voice was somber. "Maybe not," he said gently. "Some things are tough even for Santa." He slid a gentle arm around the child's shoulders. "But I'll certainly try. Why don't you tell me anyway, Peggy, just in case?"

The child sent a swift look up at her mother, then hid her face against his soft velvet sleeve. But her voice was clear. "I want you to bring a job for my mommy."

Brandi's heart squeezed painfully.

The woman looked down at her shoes. Brandi noticed that the toes were wet through. "I made the mistake of telling Peggy there won't be a Christmas at our house this year because I don't have a job. It's all she's thought of since. I'm sorry she's bothered you with it." The quiet dignity in her voice made Brandi ache even more.

Zack seemed to be utterly speechless.

He ought to have known better than that, Brandi thought. Now he'd gotten himself into a prize jam, with his big ideas about how easy it was to play Santa Claus. "That," she said under her breath, "is why we have rules."

Zack looked up at her innocently, as if he hadn't heard a word. "Brandi, didn't you say you needed floor clerks?"

"I may have. But—"

The woman interrupted. "Please. Don't trouble yourselves any further. Peggy, come along." She tugged the child gently toward the car.

Brandi scowled at Zack. Then she took one more good look at the woman and said, "Wait!" She reached into her handbag for a business card and a pen, and wrote across the top of the card, *Please do your best to find a position for . . .* "Ma'am? What's your name?"

The woman told her, with obvious reluctance. "Theresa Howard."

Brandi jotted the name on the card and handed it over. "Bring this to the third floor of Tyler-Royale tomorrow, and ask to see the personnel director."

The woman's eyes widened as she read the card. "Oh, Miss Ogilvie . . ."

For an instant, Brandi was afraid the woman was going to kiss her hand. "It will probably just be for the season," she said hastily. "But it will help."

Zack didn't say a word. They stood together in the snow until Theresa Howard and her daughter reached their car, and then started walking toward the far side of the parking lot again.

Brandi finally broke the silence. "There's no need to thank me for making you look good, Zack." She didn't look at him.

"I wasn't exactly planning to."

"Oh, you weren't?" Brandi stopped and faced him squarely, her hands on her hips. "How dare you put me in that position?"

"I didn't put you in any position. I just asked a question."

"You embarrassed me."

"Maybe I did. I'll admit I intended to. But I certainly didn't force you to hire her."

Brandi glared at him. "Well, at least you realize that much, so don't get any crazy ideas for the future. I do happen to need floor help, and Mrs. Howard looked like a good possibility. But that doesn't mean I'm going to start rescuing you if you make a habit of this."

"Of course you won't," Zack said.

Brandi thought he sounded just a little too agreeable, and she shot a suspicious stare at him. He looked perfectly innocent.

"That kind of situation is why you need training," she pointed out. "Which is what I tried to tell you the first day, when you insisted this was such an easy job. The very idea of promising a child something without any idea of what she's going to ask—don't you even realize the damage you could do?"

"I didn't promise the child anything except that I'd try," Zack argued. "I certainly didn't tell her I could give her whatever she wanted."

Brandi thought it over and decided reluctantly that perhaps he was right—technically, at least. Still, he hadn't exactly used good sense.

He'd walked on, and she had to scramble a little in the snow to catch up. "You ought to know better than to plunge in like that and meddle, Zack. The mother clearly didn't want you to interfere."

Zack stopped walking and looked down at her. In the yellowish glare of the lights, his suit had an orange cast, and his eyes were darker than she'd ever seen them before.

"You know what I think?" His voice was light, almost careless—but there was an edge to it that made Brandi uneasy. "I suspect you're really not a person at all, *Ms.* Ogilvie. You're an alien. Or a machine. That's it—you're a robot. Unfeeling and inexhaustible. And I know just the way to prove it."

Before Brandi could do more than blink in surprise, he'd swooped on her. He seized her shoulders and pulled her against him so fast and so tightly that the air was forced out of her lungs with a whoosh. She tried to push away from him, and looked up into his face to protest. But even if she'd had the breath to speak, she wouldn't have been able to, for his mouth came down on hers in a forceful, demanding kiss.

Brandi stopped fighting. She intended to stay still for a few seconds, to allow him to think she'd capitulated, though she was really waiting for a chance to break free. If he relaxed his hold for just an instant... But his arms were like iron around her, and his mouth on hers was taut and fierce and searing.

And infinitely more exciting than anything she had ever experienced before. The beard he wore was soft as silk against her skin, and he tasted of coffee and citrus, and of something incredibly sweet....

Slowly, the anger seemed to drain out of him, and his kiss gentled and softened. At the same time, it became more terrifying—for as the element of force vanished, Brandi felt herself responding to his caress. Her lips softened to welcome him, and she pressed herself to him almost against her will.

Eventually he stopped kissing her, eased her head down on his shoulder, and laid his cheek against her hair. Brandi didn't want to admit that it was probably a good thing he hadn't let go of her; her knees were too weak to support her.

Still, after an episode like that, she could hardly stand there in the man's arms and not make an effort to assert herself. "I'll accept your apology now, Zack." Her voice shook, despite her best efforts.

"Will you?" He sounded a little odd, too, as if he couldn't quite get his breath. "Then of course I'll apologize. My way."

His hand cupped her chin, and turned her face very gently up to his. This kiss started out differently—soft and easy and tender—but it didn't stay that way, and by the time he'd finished, Brandi's heart was pounding at a threatening rate, and her breath was coming in sharp gasps.

Zack held her just a little way from him, to look down at her. Unable to face him, Brandi let her head droop.

"I must admit," he said huskily, "you sure don't kiss like a robot."

Slowly he released her, keeping a hand on her shoulder for a moment till she was able to steady herself. Brandi took a step toward her car and stumbled over something in the snow at her feet. She was too rattled even to think what it could be, till Zack bent to pick up the handbag she'd dropped. He brushed the snow off the leather and gave it back to her silently. Then he took her arm so she wouldn't trip again, and started toward her car.

The silence that surrounded them was complete, as if they were caught in a bubble, shut off from the outside world. There should have been traffic noises, and sirens, and voices. But Brandi could hear nothing save the beat of her heart and the whisper of their footsteps in the snow.

"What would you have done if I hadn't bailed you out?" she said.

For a few steps she thought Zack hadn't heard her. "Is that why you hired her?" he said. His voice sounded as if it came from a distance. "To bail me out?"

"Of course not. I told you, I need floor help." She didn't look at him. Instead she fumbled for her car keys.

Zack took them and unlocked the door. "Why do you want me to think you're heartless?"

Brandi slid into the driver's seat. She'd have closed the door, but Zack—absentmindedly, no doubt—was standing in the way. "I don't see that I have a lot to do with forming your opinions," she said. "And I must say it wasn't very nice of you to look so terribly astonished because I found her a job."

Suddenly Zack smiled, and the lights were back in his eyes, dancing wickedly. "I was only startled that you didn't crush her for calling you Miss instead of Ms."

"Go home," Brandi said tartly. "You're going to freeze to death."

"Yeah," Zack mused. "Good idea. I'm going to have a hot shower. Then I'm going to open a cold beer and put my feet up and think about everything I learned today." He leaned into the car and drew a fingertip down her cheek. "And I do mean *everything*."

CHAPTER FOUR

THE snow was falling harder by the time Brandi reached her apartment complex, and her car slid a little as she tried to maneuver it into a parking spot. At the rate the flakes were coming down, they'd have a lot more than a half inch on the ground by morning. So much for Zack claiming credit for giving Brandi her Christmas wish...

"I am not going to think about him," she muttered as she closed the door of her apartment behind her. She was off duty now; she'd simply forget about Tyler-Royale's problems till morning. And, after all, Zack was a store problem.

He certainly wasn't a *personal* one.

Brandi kicked off her wet shoes and flipped through the mail—three bills, a letter from a friend, and a catalog of exotic Christmas candies and nuts, which she dropped straight into the nearest wastebasket. Then she went along the hall to her bedroom to change clothes. As soon as she'd traded her suit for jeans and a sweater and put on her warmest wool socks, she could feel the tension of the day begin to drain out of her.

She took her hair down from the tight French braid and brushed it till it gleamed. Then she dropped her gold button earrings into her jewelry case and tugged the diamond cluster from the ring finger of her left hand.

"Is there a Mr. Ogilvie?" Zack Forrest had asked yesterday. Brandi could still hear the rich undercurrents of his voice echoing through her mind and making her feel warm and cold all at the same time.

It was a question Brandi hadn't expected. She'd been wearing this ring for two years now, and it had been a long time since anyone had actually questioned her about its meaning. Many people seemed to think it was a wedding ring, but that she didn't make a big thing of it because she preferred to keep her private life to herself. And as long as they didn't come straight out and ask, Brandi had never felt obliged to confide the truth.

She had never gone to any particular trouble to promote the illusion that she was married. The ring had been a reward to herself when she'd successfully completed her management training course and been assigned a store of her own, and it had never occurred to her that some people might think it resembled a wedding ring. Brandi didn't think it did; the center stone was much larger than the other gems, with a narrow band of diamonds below it and a sort of starburst above, and it had always looked to Brandi like the dinner ring it was.

But it was funny how suggestible people were. To some of them, any ring worn on the left hand must stand for a relationship. And when Brandi consistently came alone to company functions, never appeared anywhere with a date, and didn't invite anyone to her home—well, maybe it wasn't unreasonable for her employees to assume she was married, but her husband was some kind of hermit.

Brandi didn't mind. A woman's life was a whole lot less complicated when no one worried about her single status or tried to match her up with the right man. That was particularly true for a woman at management level, one who spent most of her waking hours involved with her career. It was dangerous for such a woman to date a man who worked for her—and where else was she likely to run into one, when she had so little time for pursuits outside her profession?

Not that Brandi had bothered to think that argument all the way through, because it held no importance for her. She had no interest in adding a man to her life. A relationship only complicated things; she'd learned that lesson long ago.

So why had she reacted so strongly to Zack Forrest tonight?

Just asking the question brought back tinges of the breathless, achy, almost dizzy feeling that had swept over her as he kissed her tonight in the parking lot. She told herself that her reaction was easily explained; the man had practically assaulted her, so it was no wonder she'd felt breathless and achy and dizzy.

But she couldn't quite explain why she'd eventually kissed him back. Why she'd clung to him. Why she hadn't given him the sock in the jaw that he deserved.

A tinge of loneliness, that was all, she decided. No matter how happy she was with her life—and most of the time she was quite satisfied—still, she was alone a great deal of the time. At the store she was surrounded by people, but apart from Casey Amos, Brandi had been careful not to make those people her friends. A manager had to keep a little distance from her employees in order to be effective.

And at home... Sometimes, she admitted, her own footsteps sounded loud in the quiet apartment, and sometimes it was a temptation to talk to herself just to hear a voice.

So perhaps it was no wonder that tonight, once Zack had stopped trying to prove his point, she'd gotten caught up in the moment. One thing she had to admit—the man certainly knew how to kiss.

But it wasn't going to happen again. Now that she was aware and on her guard—

The doorbell rang, and Brandi sighed and went to answer it. If it was Zack, she decided, she'd kick him in the kneecap and slam the door in his face.

But it wasn't Zack; her visitors were three preadolescent girls selling holiday garlands to raise money for their school club. "We took orders back in October," one of them explained, "but you weren't at home. Now we've got an extra garland, and we thought you might like to buy it. Since you don't seem to have any other Christmas decorations..."

Brandi said, "I don't have decorations because I don't want them, and I don't want a garland, either. Look, I admire your efforts, and I'll happily make a donation to your club, but the garland would be wasted on me. So give it to someone who'll get some good out of it, all right?" She wrote a check and closed the door with relief. At least that had been easily dealt with. If it had been Zack, on the other hand...

And just why had she jumped to the conclusion it might be Zack at her door? That made no sense at all. If the man had anything else to say, he'd surely have said it in the parking lot. Only an idiot would even dream that he might follow her home. By now he was enjoying his shower, or perhaps he'd progressed as far as the cold beer.

"And whatever he might be doing," Brandi said, "it certainly holds no fascination for me!"

It wasn't as if she wanted him around, that was sure.

The snowy streets slowed her down the next morning, and the regular monthly meeting of the store's employee association had already started when Brandi came in. Every chair and sofa in the second-floor furniture department was lined with employees. Many were ready for work when the store opened in an hour; others were in casual clothes because they were scheduled for the evening shift or had the day off. Brandi was still amazed, when she saw them all together, at how many people it took to run a store the size of Tyler-Royale.

Today's crowd was smaller than usual, however. The snow had continued through the night, and traffic was a mess. That, plus the longer-than-normal hours they'd all been putting in, had probably kept some of the off-duty employees from making the effort to attend so early in the morning. And the flu continued to be a worry; yesterday they'd had a dozen employees call in sick. Brandi wondered what the report would look like today.

She didn't realize she was looking for Zack till she found him, and then—when he met her gaze and smiled at her—she could have kicked herself. But in fact, it would have been hard to miss him; he was ready for work, and the red suit he wore, contrasted with the big, dark green wing chair he'd chosen, seemed to cry out for attention.

This morning his white Santa beard lay on his knee. Brandi wondered if he'd left it off because there would be no children here, or because it made his face itch. It was funny that she'd hardly noticed the beard last night, except for that sensation of silky smoothness as he kissed her....

And that, she told herself, is quite enough of that. She had far better things to think about than what had happened last night.

She didn't smile back at him. Zack made a show of pulling up his sleeve to check his watch, and he shook his head sorrowfully at her for being late.

Brandi scowled at him, leaned against a pillar at the side of the room, and tried to pretend Zack Forrest didn't exist. But it took effort to focus her attention on Casey Amos, who stood in the center of the room as she conducted the meeting, and a few minutes later Brandi found her gaze drifting toward Zack once more.

He caught her eye and pantomimed an invitation for her to come over.

Brandi suspected he intended to invite her to sit on the arm of his chair. Wouldn't that look cozy, she thought, and shook her head. Then she moved to the back of the room and leaned against a big armoire.

Casey said, "Those of you who want to take part in the employee gift exchange should put your names in the box in the lounge by next Monday."

One of the customer service representatives hurried in, looking a little frazzled. Zack waved her over and stood up, offering his chair.

"On Tuesday," Casey went on, "everyone who's put in a name will draw one out, and the exchange will be at the party on the following Sunday night."

Zack looked around the room, then lazily headed for Brandi's armoire.

Brandi's heartbeat speeded up just a little in anticipation of being close to him once more. Don't be silly, she told herself. What happened last night had been an aberration, born of mutual irritation and frustration, and it was over. She shouldn't be having any feelings about him at all.

Casey didn't appear to have her mind completely on what she was doing. Her gaze seemed to shift from Brandi to Zack, and then back to Brandi once more.

Her interest didn't necessarily mean anything, Brandi thought. That red suit was hard to ignore, and it must look to Casey as if the man was walking out of the meeting. Even with her eyes fixed on Casey, Brandi couldn't quite avoid seeing Zack at the edge of her peripheral vision, coming steadily closer. No wonder Casey was looking at him.

"Five-dollar limit, just like last year," Casey went on, and glanced at the sheaf of notes in her hand. "The party will be downstairs in the atrium, with music by..."

Brandi tuned her out. The annual Christmas party was just one more nuisance in an already over-busy season, in her opinion. She wouldn't go at all except that it would hurt her employees' feelings if she didn't show up.

Zack appeared beside her. "Avoiding me?" he said softly.

He looked very comfortable, with his arms folded and his shoulder against the door of the armoire, right next to Brandi.

"I beg your pardon?"

"You heard me. You're avoiding me."

"Of course I'm not."

"Then why didn't you come over and sit down? I'm a gentleman. I'd have given you my chair. Or are you so firm a feminist that you wouldn't take it?"

"I'm only an honorary member of the employee association, so I try to stay in the background."

"Is that so? Don't you believe in clubs, either?"

"It's not a club, Zack. Since technically I don't work for the store itself but for the corporation that owns the chain, I'm really not eligible to belong to the employee association. But they invited me to join anyway."

He grinned. "I'll bet that made your day—being asked to join the play group."

Brandi tried to ignore him. It was difficult, he was close enough that the barest hint of his cologne—very light, very appealing—tickled her nose.

"Or did you think I might kiss you again?" Zack murmured. "Was that what scared you off? Let me assure you, I wouldn't."

"I should certainly hope not."

"Not in public, at any rate. In private, on the other hand, you could probably tempt me."

Brandi's jaw dropped and she turned to face him directly. "Touch me again," she warned, "and you'll be out on your ear—Ross Clayton's friend or not. Got that straight, Forrest?"

Zack didn't turn a hair. "I'll try to keep it in mind." He settled both shoulders against the armoire and looked out over the room. He was so close that Brandi could feel the heat of his body, but she knew if she moved, he'd understand perfectly well why she'd done so, and he'd be amused. And Brandi was just stubborn enough to refuse to give him the satisfaction.

She put her chin up, folded her arms in imitation of his pose, and turned her attention back to Casey Amos. Why in heaven's name wasn't the woman moving the meeting along? she wondered. They didn't have all day. Despite the snow, there'd be customers arriving in a few minutes. But there stood Casey staring at her....

Brandi swallowed hard and tried to imagine what that exchange had looked like from across the room. The only good news she could think of was that they were at the back of the room, so only Casey had been in a position to see much. At least, she hoped everyone else had kept their backs turned.

Casey cleared her throat and flipped to the next page of her notes. "We're going to need more volunteers than usual to help with the Wishing Tree. We've had six families register in the first week of the program, but then Pat Emerson got the flu and things have come to a screeching halt."

Brandi frowned. Pat was ill? That must have happened just yesterday, or surely she'd have heard it before now.

"What's the Wishing Tree?" Zack asked under his breath.

Brandi would have liked to ignore him, but that would no doubt be just about as effective as pretending an impacted wisdom tooth didn't hurt. "You've noticed the Christmas trees in the atrium?"

"They're a little hard to overlook. A dozen of them, each ten feet tall—"

"Most of them are just to set the mood for the store and show off special merchandise. But one is the Wishing Tree. Families who can't afford clothes and toys and special things for Christmas ask for what they'd like to have, and the wishes are hung on the tree. Then customers or employees pick out the person they'd like to shop for and buy the gifts."

Zack frowned. "You just let people walk in and hang their wishes on the tree? You've never struck me as such a trusting sort before, Brandi."

"Of course there are restrictions. In the first place, there aren't any names on the trees, just ages and sizes, and the customer service department takes charge of the gifts and delivers them to the right people. They also make sure the family is genuinely in need. People have to be registered with a charitable organization before they're eligible for the Wishing Tree. That's what Pat Emerson was doing before she got sick—coordinating all those details."

"Who's going to do it now?"

"I don't know." Brandi was racking her brain, without success. "Pat will be hard to replace. It takes a special kind of person to do that job—warm and insightful and empathetic, without being a pushover."

Zack shrugged. "Sounds like a management sort of problem to me."

"Management? If you're implying that I should take it over, Zack, let me assure you—"

"That you haven't the qualifications? I'm not surprised you'd say that. You might not actually be a robot, but—"

"What I haven't got is the time," Brandi pointed out.

Casey went on, "At least one person in every department should try to stay familiar with the needs listed on the tree in order to help shoppers. And if anyone can volunteer to fill in for Pat till she's back in shape, I'd love to stick around after the meeting and talk to you."

Zack raised a hand to draw Casey's attention.

"It takes a lot of time," Brandi warned. "Pat devoted herself to that project."

"Time I've got plenty of. Since I have to be here anyway, waiting around for my various shifts, I might as well be doing something constructive."

Brandi bit her tongue to keep from reminding him that she had offered to amend his working hours. "I should also warn you," she went on, "that Pat—"

Zack looked down at her, his eyes wide and looking even darker than usual, and interrupted. "Are you trying to stop me from doing a good deed, Ms. Ogilvie? It's bad enough that you're a Scrooge yourself, but to stand in someone else's way..."

Brandi gritted her teeth.

Zack raised his voice. "I'll volunteer."

Casey peered at him. "Hey, that's great. Stick around after the meeting—I'll get Pat's files, and Ms. Ogilvie will fill you in on the details." She turned to the next order of business.

Brandi looked straight ahead and waited.

A full minute went by before Zack said with deceptive gentleness, "What exactly did she mean, you'll fill me in on the details?"

"Pat was coordinating the program, but I'm in charge of the Wishing Tree. It's not just a store project, it's a corporate one—there are Wishing Trees through the whole chain."

"I'm going to be working directly with you?"

The look on his face, Brandi thought, almost made up for the certain irritation of having to work with him for the next week or two, till Pat was back to full capacity. "I tried to tell you before you committed yourself," she said sweetly. "But of course it wouldn't have made a difference to you, would it? Since it's all in a good cause, I mean."

The meeting was finally over just minutes before the store opened, and employees rushed off in all directions. Brandi waited till the confusion had eased before she tried to catch Casey. "How long has Pat been ill?"

"Several days. Don't look at me like that, Brandi. I only heard it myself this morning, or I'd have told you. She had a couple of regular days off, and she thought she'd be over the flu in time to come back as scheduled."

"That's going to create a major problem with the Wishing Tree."

"Oh, I don't know. I imagine your Santa can handle anything he puts his mind to." Casey looked up at Zack and smiled. "It's the hole in my department I'm not sure I can fill—Pat's my best saleswoman." She put a hand on Zack's sleeve. "Let me give you just the highlights on the responsibilities. It's not difficult, really, once you get the hang of it, and I'm sure Brandi will—"

Just then, the clerk from Salon Elegance who had taken care of Brandi's mustard-stained blouse came up to her and held out a Tyler-Royale bag, and Brandi couldn't hear what Casey was saying about her. It was probably just as well; Brandi suspected she wouldn't have liked the program Casey was mapping out for her.

"Sorry, Ms. Ogilvie," the clerk said. "The cleaners did the best they could, but you can see they weren't very successful."

Brandi pulled the blouse out of the bag. It was perfectly pressed and neatly folded, but on the front was still an unmistakable blotchy yellow stain.

She thanked the clerk for trying, then crumpled the blouse into the bag and tucked it under her arm. But Casey had finished her instructions by that time, and Zack was fiddling with his long white beard, getting it anchored just right before he went over to Santa's Workshop.

"Was that a favorite blouse?" he asked. "It looks like it had a bath in mustard."

"It did, as a matter of fact," Brandi said. "And since you were the cause of its ruin, I'm tempted to take the price of it out of your pay. So if you're wise—"

"Me?" Zack sounded shocked. "How could I have caused that?"

"It happened the first time you showed up here, when my secretary paged me to come and talk to you, so technically you're responsible."

"Technically?" Zack started to smile. "Now why doesn't it surprise me at all that you'd think that way?"

The long white beard hid the dimple in his cheek, but Brandi knew precisely where it was. Suddenly she found herself wanting to slip a fingertip under the edge of the soft, fluffy whiskers and touch that tiny hidden spot. And then she wanted to tug the beard away so the dimple wasn't hidden anymore, so she could kiss it...kiss him...once more.

The desire was so strong, so sudden, and so irrational that she was having trouble breathing. What's happening to you, Brandi Ogilvie? she asked herself. You've lost your mind entirely, that's what!

"Don't you think you'd better get to work?" Her voice was a bit sharp.

"Yes, ma'am," Zack murmured. "Or I won't have enough of a paycheck for you to dock."

Brandi didn't watch him walk away. She didn't have to; she knew without even looking that he was in no apparent hurry. The public address system came to life with a crackle, followed by the opening note of "Jingle Bells." The mercilessly cheery sound was enough to push Brandi over the brink.

She squared her shoulders and turned to Casey. "By the way, would you kindly stop calling him *my* Santa?"

Casey's eyebrows soared. "Well, he does seem to be sticking rather close to you, don't you think?"

Brandi gave it up. Further protest would only call more attention to the situation than she wanted, and she'd already said more than her ordinary good sense would have allowed her to.

"I'd better get downstairs," Casey murmured. "Unless the snow keeps people away, I'm going to need six arms today."

"I might have a new employee for you."

"Joy," Casey said without enthusiasm. "Just what I need—someone to train."

"It'll make your time go faster," Brandi said with mock sympathy. "I'll tell the personnel director to send her down to you if she shows up."

"*If*? You mean you haven't actually hired her?"

"Not yet. It's a long story."

"I wish I had time to listen to it," Casey admitted. She started to walk away.

"Wait a minute," Brandi said. "Where'd you get that button?"

Casey fingered her lapel, where a small plastic-covered badge nestled discreetly against the white carnation that marked her as a department manager. "You mean this one?"

"Of course I mean that one."

Casey cupped a protective hand around the button so Brandi couldn't see it clearly. "Zack gave it to me this morning."

"I should have known Zack would be behind this. What's it about anyway?"

"You mean you haven't approved it? As cozy as the two of you have been—"

"Cozy?" Brandi's voice would have turned antifreeze to slush. "Give it here."

"Come on, Brandi, it's just a fun little gimmick."

"You know political buttons and protest ribbons and all those sorts of personal statements are forbidden in this store."

"This is hardly a political announcement, and you can't have my button. If you want one, go ask Zack— I'm sure he'll give you one. You just have to promise you'll do something nice for someone every day till Christmas, and he'll make you an official Santa's Friend, too. Look, I've really got to run—we wouldn't want to lose sales because the department's not open, would we?" She was gone—still wearing the button—before Brandi could object.

Brandi stalked across the second floor to Santa's Workshop. There were no children in line; nevertheless she firmly set the "Santa's Feeding His Reindeer" sign in place and closed the gate just in case someone came along before she'd finished with her errant Santa.

Zack had propped one elbow on the arm of the big chair and stretched his long legs out as if he was admiring the high polish on the toes of his boots. As she approached, he rolled his eyes and stood up. "Ms. Ogilvie," he said in a tone of long-suffering patience, "at this rate, the reindeer are going to be too fat to fly."

"Then we'll make venison sausage of them and you can ride the subway and the El on Christmas Eve," Brandi snapped.

Zack sighed. "You know, I have this instinctive feeling you're unhappy with me. What is it now?"

"You mean there's more going on than just the buttons?"

"You're unhappy about the buttons?" He sounded incredulous.

"Not the buttons themselves. It's a cute gag. But you can't just start that kind of gimmick without consulting me. There's a policy in the chain that no employee can wear political or religious jewelry or buttons—"

Zack's eyebrows almost disappeared under the white fur band of his velvet cap. "So which category do you put Santa's Friends in?"

"It's the principle of the thing, Zack! If one kind of personal statement is allowed, where do you draw the line? What about black arm bands? Protest signs?"

"Has anyone ever told you you're a little intense, Brandi?" He shook his head as if in confusion. "And here I thought you were upset because I rearranged Toyland last night."

Brandi was speechless. "You did *what*?"

"Only a couple of the game displays. I got bored with shopping, you see, so I was just looking at the toys. Some of the shelves were too crowded, and it was hard to get one box out of the stack. I just moved them around so—"

"That's it," Brandi said. "You're done. You're fired."

Zack looked at her for a few seconds in silence. "Over a few buttons?"

"No. I'm terminating you because you're meddling in areas that are none of your concern. You were hired to be a Santa, not the manager of this store."

Zack pulled what looked like a television remote control out of the capacious pocket of his jacket.

"What's that?" Brandi asked.

"A cellular phone. You know, you can use it anywhere. It comes in very handy when Santa needs to consult the main data banks at the North Pole."

"Funny. What are you doing?"

"Well, I don't need to ask the elves whether you've been nice or naughty this year. I can draw my own conclusions. So I'm going to call Ross so you can tell him yourself why I don't seem to be working out." He punched a string of numbers and held the phone out to her.

"Dammit, Zack—"

The phone's buzz gave way to silence, and then to Ross Clayton's voice. It didn't surprise Brandi that there was a private number that rang directly into Ross Clayton's downtown office, bypassing switchboards and secretaries, but it startled her that Zack had it. Brandi had never been offered that kind of access; all her calls to the CEO took the standard route.

She glared at Zack, and then at the phone. He continued to silently hold it out to her, and eventually she took it. "Ross? It's Brandi Ogilvie."

"I'm glad you called. I've been wanting to talk to you."

"Have you?"

"Yes. Zack tells me he's thrilled with the cooperation he's getting from the whole store, especially you. From what I hear, things must be working out great."

Zack was looking at her with wide-eyed innocence, as if he could hear the entire conversation.

Ross went on, "Of course I could see that for myself when I was in the store last night."

"You were here?" Brandi's voice was little more than a gasp. "When? You didn't stop in the office."

"Oh, it was the middle of the evening. You'd probably been at home for hours."

Last evening, she thought. Before closing time. Before that kiss in the parking lot.

"Kelly and I brought the kids over to visit Santa. Not Zack, of course—they'd have been onto him in a second—so we waited till the next one came on duty. But afterward he was telling me how much he's enjoying himself."

"I'll bet he told you all this while he was rearranging the displays in Toyland," Brandi said dryly, and waited for the reaction. Surely Ross wouldn't condone this takeover, no matter how good a friend Zack seemed to be.

"As a matter of fact, yes—that was what he was doing. It looked pretty good when he was done. The department manager seemed to like the new look, too."

Brandi's head was swimming.

"And the Santa's Friend buttons are cute. Which reminds me, I haven't done my good deed for the day yet. So what's on your mind? Surely you're not canceling out of the party now."

"The Christmas party? No," Brandi said weakly. "I'll be there."

"Good. I know Whitney's looking forward to seeing you. In fact, I think you're the main reason she's coming this year. What can I do for you, Brandi?"

"I was just..." She hesitated. "I called to tell you Zack's the most...innovative employee I've had in some time."

Ross laughed heartily. "Now that doesn't surprise me. Take good care of him, and keep in touch, all right? I'll see you Saturday night."

"Sure." She didn't meet Zack's eyes as she handed the phone back to him.

He punched the cutoff button and dropped the phone into his pocket without a comment.

Brandi gathered her dignity. "I may have acted a little too hastily."

Zack looked astounded. "*You*, Ms. Ogilvie?"

"Don't rub it in, Forrest."

"So that means I still have a job?"

"If I were you, I wouldn't take on any long-term debts," Brandi snapped. "But for the moment—yes, you still have a job." She stalked toward the gate and set the sign aside.

"Oh, Brandi," Zack called.

She didn't turn around. "What is it now?"

"Did I hear you say you're going to the Claytons' Christmas party Saturday night?"

"Yes. Why?"

"So am I," Zack said easily. "How would you like to go with me?"

CHAPTER FIVE

BRANDI considered picking up the "Santa's Feeding His Reindeer" sign and hitting Zack over the head with it. She settled for saying, as evenly as she could manage, "No, thank you."

"Parties like that are a lot more fun when you have a date," he pointed out.

"I happen to already *have* a date," she snapped. Her arrangement with Whitney Townsend might not be quite the kind of date Zack was thinking of, but in Brandi's opinion it was just as important—and more enjoyable, too.

Zack didn't answer. That made Brandi nervous, and finally, unable to control her curiosity, she turned around to face him. He was looking at her with what appeared to be amazement.

Brandi was annoyed. "You don't need to look astonished about it."

"I'm not astonished. I'm merely overwhelmed by disappointment." He didn't sound particularly discouraged, though. He went on blithely, "Well, that'll teach me to ask earlier. About this Wishing Tree business..."

"What about it?"

"I'll be off duty most of the afternoon. Shall we have lunch and you can tell me all about it?"

"I expect to be very busy this afternoon." If the tone of her voice didn't freeze him out, she thought, nothing would.

It didn't. "How about later, then? I'll do my din-
nertime stint and we can spend the evening on the
Wishing Tree."

"I hardly think it will take all evening."

Zack grinned. "Oh, in that case," he said, "we can
use the rest of the time to get to know each other. Won't
that be fun?"

Brandi finished analyzing November's sales figures and
signed the final report for Dora to fax to the main offices
downtown in the morning. It was well past six, and Dora
would have gone home by now.

Or perhaps she wouldn't wait for morning and her
secretary—almost every department in the store was
running slightly ahead of her projections, and that was
the kind of news Brandi always liked to share.

She was surprised at the time. It seemed she'd been
occupied with the sales reports for no more than an hour,
but the whole afternoon had sped by while she worked.
And there hadn't been a word from Zack. Maybe he'd
had to be on duty at Santa's Workshop later than he
expected. Or maybe he'd decided they didn't need this
little heart-to-heart chat after all. Wishful thinking, she
chided herself.

Brandi was startled to find Dora still at her desk, which
was covered with the advertising layouts that would run
in the next few weeks. Brandi checked her watch again
to be sure she hadn't misread the time. "What are you
still doing here, Dora?"

"You told me not to interrupt you this afternoon,"
Dora said comfortably.

"For heaven's sake, I didn't mean you couldn't go
home when you were finished with your work!"

"But I'm not finished. Besides, your Santa—"

Brandi frowned a little.

Very smoothly, Dora went on, "I mean, Mr. Forrest was in. I told him I had orders not to disturb you, and he waited for a while."

"And then he just went away? You amaze me."

"He said he'd be in Toyland where he could do something constructive while he waited."

"I suppose that means he's rearranging the whole department."

"He didn't say what he intended to do. At any rate, I was afraid if I left he'd sneak back up here and barge in on you, so I stayed. The advertising slicks needed sorting anyway."

"Thanks, Dora. I don't deserve such loyalty." Brandi handed over the sales report. "Would you fax this downtown? And then just leave the rest of the advertising—tomorrow's soon enough to finish it."

She took the escalator down to the second floor. The store wasn't crowded; the snowstorm was over, but the aftereffects were still keeping many people at home, just as she'd predicted. Till the streets were completely cleared, Christmas shopping would suffer. At least the season was still only halfway along; this kind of storm just a few days before the holiday could cripple the store's bottom line.

Her favorite Santa, the one with the half glasses, was holding court by the Workshop, and Brandi paused for a moment to admire him in action. It wasn't that Zack was out of place in that chair, exactly; he did just fine— far better, she had to admit, than she'd originally hoped for. But she'd prided herself for years on perfect Santas like this one. He looked so at ease, so natural, so comfortable in the big chair....

Except he wasn't sitting in the regular Santa chair, but in a dark green wing one—the chair Zack had been occupying this morning up in the furniture department during the employee meeting, and then had given up to the woman who'd come in late. Brandi didn't want to think about how he'd managed to talk the department manager into letting him requisition it. Or maybe he'd just moved it over to Toyland without anyone's approval....

Santa looked up from the child in his lap and called, "Thanks, Ms. Ogilvie! It was very thoughtful of you to change the chairs. I really appreciate a comfortable seat—you know, those packs of toys are heavy, and I have to take care of my back." He turned his attention once more to the child.

Brandi didn't bother to tell him she'd had nothing to do with the chair. She just waved and went on into Toyland.

She almost tripped over Zack; he was siting cross-legged in the middle of an aisle with a couple of youngsters, and they'd spread the pieces of a train layout all over the floor. The kids were assembling the wooden track while Zack took the engines and cars out of the box.

Brandi leaned against a case full of fashion dolls. "Zack, what are you doing?"

He looked up. "Demonstrating the flexibility and creativity of this particular model of train kit."

"It looks to me as if you're playing."

"Well, yes," Zack admitted.

"I thought so."

"That's part of what makes this a very special toy, you understand. It not only captures the imagination of children and releases their creative side, it intrigues adults, as well."

Brandi ignored the nods of the man and woman—obviously the children's parents—who were standing nearby. "You're sure you're not just talking about *some* adults?"

"If you're implying I'm a case of arrested development—"

"Well, I don't see a lot of men your age sitting on the floor playing with wooden trains. Is this the height of your ambition, Zack?"

"Of course not." The track was assembled; Zack set the train down on it and leaned back against the nearest display case while the kids took over. "I hope someday I'll be sitting on the floor playing with trains with my own kids."

Suddenly Brandi could almost see that picture. A towering Christmas tree loaded with lights, a pile of packages, a train spread out on the floor, a couple of pajama-clad youngsters—and Zack.

Brandi shook her head in amazement. The man was hypnotic; she didn't even like Christmas, but he could still evoke in her mind an image straight out of Norman Rockwell. She could almost smell the turkey cooking.

She was annoyed with herself, and so her tone was sharp. "I thought you said you wanted to take care of the Wishing Tree business tonight."

"You'll have to pardon me for keeping you waiting." He didn't sound in the least sorry. "Of course, the dragon on your office doorstep left me kicking my heels for half an hour without even telling you I was there— but I'm sure you can explain to me how that's different."

"Dora's not a dragon. She just knew I was very busy this afternoon."

"Right." Zack stood up. "I'll be with you in a minute. Let me check with the department manager first."

"Why?"

"To make sure he can do without me. It's not terribly busy just now, but he's short a couple of clerks tonight—the flu got them. In the meantime, why don't you go get your coat?''

''What for?''

''Because I'm taking you out for a sandwich or something.''

Brandi started to protest, but she realized abruptly that she was hungry. Still, there was something uncomfortable about going out with him. ''Let's just go to the tearoom.''

Zack shook his head. ''Now that you've broken your self-imposed isolation, everyone in the store probably wants to talk to you.''

''And you want me all to yourself?'' Brandi's voice was saccharine. ''How charming!''

Zack's eyebrows lifted slightly. ''It's not that. I just don't care to risk you being paged. You might spray mustard all over me this time, and I'm particularly fond of this sweater.''

Brandi could understand that sentiment; today he was wearing hunter green cashmere.

Before she could open her mouth to argue, however, he'd vanished toward the cash register, and by the time he returned she'd thought better of her insistence on the tearoom. It was handy, yes—but the last thing she needed was for another dozen employees to see them together and draw their own conclusions. Besides, though Tyler-Royale food was good, during this season she seldom had time to go anywhere else, and she knew the menus of both the tearoom and the cafeteria by heart. So she went meekly back to her office to get her coat and boots, and met Zack by the employee exit.

The parking lot had been plowed, and the snow that remained underfoot was polished smooth by traffic. But in areas where the snow lay as nature had intended, the crystals caught the lights and sparkled as if a generous hand had scattered diamonds across the soft-sculptured drifts.

"My car or yours?" she asked outside the employee exit.

"Mine's no doubt closer." He showed her to a dark sedan not far from the store.

The car was covered with snow, so Brandi couldn't tell much about it. But she looked thoughtfully at the distinctive trademark embossed into the leather seats, and listened to the soft purr of the engine coming to life. "You know, Zack, when Ross asked me to hire you, he said you'd been having some tough times lately."

"Oh, I have." His voice was emphatic. "Yes. Very tough."

"Obviously he didn't mean financially."

"What makes you think that?"

"I'm not an idiot, Zack. That Santa suit of yours is velvet, and the boots are top-grain leather—"

"Rented," Zack said succinctly.

"You're carrying a cellular phone. That's not an inexpensive toy."

He shrugged. "I'd have to buy my way out of the service contract, and that would cost as much as using it the rest of the year. I'm very careful not to exceed the amount of time my contract allows, though, so I don't have to pay extra."

"I'll bet you are. And you're driving a very nice car."

"It's the darnedest thing, but I can't afford to sell it."

"Oh, really?"

"I'm serious. You know how tough it is to get the full price out of a new car. Once you drive it off the lot, it drops ten percent in value just like that." He snapped his fingers. "So I might as well keep it for a little while."

"Till it's repossessed?" Brandi said dryly.

"If it comes to that. After all, if I sold it I couldn't clear enough to buy something else, and then how would I get around?"

"You could always use the reindeer. What are you really, Zack? A corporate spy?"

"Brandi, don't you think if Ross wanted to plant a spy in your store he could have hidden me better than this?"

"I wasn't thinking of Ross."

Zack grinned. "Now that's a unique point of view. Would it make you happier if I started wearing a trench coat and dark glasses and slinking around behind displays?"

"So you're admitting it?"

"I'm not admitting anything."

"Well, if you're just a Santa, I'm—" She stopped. A half-formed suspicion stirred to life in the back of her mind, but she couldn't quite put her finger on it. Until she could think it all out, there wasn't much point in pursuing the matter. And in the meantime she was still thoroughly stuck with the man.

"As long as we're speaking of Ross," Zack went on, "are you sure you won't reconsider and go to the party with me Saturday?"

"I thought this was a corporate party," Brandi pointed out. "Last year nobody below assistant manager status was invited."

"I know. Sounds deadly dull, doesn't it—all those assistant managers drinking champagne and buttering people up?"

"So the Claytons are planning to enliven the party by including you?"

"Well, not just me, I'm sure," Zack said modestly. "A few friends here and there. You haven't answered my question, you know."

"I don't believe in breaking a date because another one comes along."

"Even if it's a better one?"

"Now that's a matter of opinion, isn't it?"

She expected he'd take offense, but he didn't seem to. "Italian food all right?"

"It's fine with me."

A couple of miles from the mall, Zack parked the car beside a restaurant and came around to open Brandi's door. "You know," he said, "I've been thinking."

"That sounds dangerous," Brandi said under her breath.

"Well, it was quiet all day. Not many kids, so I had a lot of time on my hands, even while I was occupying Santa's chair."

"Speaking of Santa's chair, Zack—"

"I know, if there's any wear on it you'll take it out of my paycheck."

"That wasn't what I meant."

"It wasn't?"

"No. I haven't sat in Santa's chair, so how would I know it's uncomfortable?"

"Didn't I tell you it was?"

"Well, maybe you did, but you've told me so many things I never know when to take you seriously. I just wish you wouldn't go off on these tangents without checking with me first. You've already got Casey starting to question policy."

"Maybe that's a good thing, if she's going to be managing a store of her own next year."

"I don't want to get into an argument with you about details, all right? The point is, I can't have every stock boy and salesclerk setting their own rules, but with you as a stunning example, I'm apt to have mutiny in the ranks by Christmas."

"Is that all that's bothering you?"

"*All*? Don't you think that's enough?"

"Well, maybe you've got a point," he conceded. "In that case—"

The hostess greeted Zack by name and showed them to a table with a checked cloth and enormous red napkins. The menus were huge, too, and seemed to list every conceivable combination of pasta and sauce. Brandi glanced at hers and put it aside. "You were saying?"

Zack looked at her over the top of his menu. "I knew you were decisive, Brandi, but really—"

"The only thing I've decided is that I'm not going to read the whole menu. Since you obviously come here often, you can choose."

"And that way you can concentrate on me," Zack mused. "What a perfectly charming—"

Brandi interrupted. "Just make it something that doesn't take hours to cook. Now I believe you were going to agree to some terms concerning your job?"

Zack held up a hand as if he was taking an oath. "I'll check out anything important with you before I do it."

Brandi supposed she'd have to be satisfied with that, inadequate as it was. What was his definition of important anyway? "All right. Now we can talk about the Wishing Tree."

"Just a minute. I want to tell you about my idea first."

Brandi looked at him a little doubtfully. "Zack—"

"You said not two minutes ago that you wanted me to consult you before I did anything else," Zack reminded her.

That does it, Brandi thought. I'm caught in my own trap. "What now?"

"Have you considered keeping the store open extremely late one night a week till Christmas, so parents can leave the kids at home and come to do their Santa shopping in peace?''

Brandi frowned. ''Can't they just get a sitter during normal hours?''

''Not as easily as they can once the kids are in bed. Besides, the kids are apt to know where they've gone, and there are boxes and bags to hide when they get back. If it's the dead of night and the little ones are asleep, it's much easier to sneak the packages in and keep the Santa myth intact.''

''How do you know so much about kids?'' Brandi challenged. ''If you don't have any of your own yet—''

''Oh, there are a dozen or so who have adopted me as their favorite honorary uncle.'' He ordered manicotti for both of them and a bottle of red wine, and leaned across the table to drape Brandi's napkin solicitously across her lap.

''And that's why you thought being a Santa would fill in an awkward spot in your life?''

''I suppose that's what brought it to mind. What do you think? Shall we organize Parents' Night Out?''

''Aren't you going to have enough to do with your job and the Wishing Tree?''

''What's to do? A little advertising, a few signs in Toyland...''

''A few employees who are disgruntled at having to work even crazier hours.''

''I don't think that will be a problem. I've talked to several, and most of them think it's a good idea.''

''And I suppose you've already mentioned it to Ross, too.''

''Well, yes. I didn't think it would hurt.''

Brandi sighed. So much for checking things out before he acted! ''Go ahead, then—ask the manager of Toyland

and see what he thinks. But you're only authorized to proceed if he wants to, and if you can get the mall management to agree to let us break the rule about normal business hours. Understand that, Zack?''

''Absolutely,'' he said airily. ''And while we're on the subject, what about a special night for senior citizens to shop? I bet they'd like not being knocked over by the regular shoppers. We could organize buses to go around and pick them up—''

''One thing at a time, Forrest. What are you doing anyway? Maneuvering for a job in public relations?''

''Now that's a thought.''

''Well, take my advice and don't settle for a single store. With all your ideas, you could keep the whole chain hopping.''

''Thank you.''

''I didn't intend it as a compliment.''

The waiter brought their wine. Zack tasted it and nodded, and the waiter filled their glasses and silently went away.

Brandi swirled her wine and sipped. ''Take those crazy buttons, for instance...''

''What about them?''

''Where did you get the things anyway?''

''The notions department made up a thousand for me. They did a good job, didn't they?'' He reached in his pocket. ''I've got an extra if you'd like it.''

''No, thanks.''

He tipped his head to one side and studied her.

''You don't think I'm capable of doing a good deed a day, do you?'' Brandi challenged.

''I'd sure like to watch you try.''

''Well, that's got nothing to do with it. There's a corporate policy that forbids wearing that kind of thing, and until it's lifted, I feel I have to abide by it—even if

I end up blinking at violations by every member of my staff."

"Ross has a button."

"I know. He told me. That's different, because Ross makes the rules."

"The idea seems to be working anyway. I just started handing the buttons out yesterday, and I think the store feels more cordial already. Everybody likes being Santa's friend, you see. I think that good feeling could transfer into the Wishing Tree program, too." He leaned forward confidingly. "We could end up with the biggest Wishing Tree program in the chain."

"It's not a competition, Zack."

"Pity. So tell me what I've let myself in for."

"Mostly a whole lot of paperwork and detail. The family comes in to talk to you. You check with the agencies to be sure they're really needy."

Zack frowned. "I can't imagine someone applying for charity if they don't need it."

"Then you'd be surprised."

"But their pride—"

"Exactly. The people who need help the worst are the ones who are too proud to ask for it."

"Like Theresa Howard," Zack said.

Brandi nodded and made a mental note to check with Casey Amos and the personnel director tomorrow about whether the woman had come in. "On the other hand, there are some who are out to get anything that's available. Pat used to spot-check some of the families whose stories sounded a little fishy—she'd go drive by the address and be sure the pieces all fit together."

"And did they?"

"Not always. But don't go on a crusade. The majority are legitimate. It's basically pretty simple. The family makes a list of their needs, and you'll fill out a star for each person and put it on the tree, with age and clothing sizes and likes and dislikes, so the person who chooses that star to shop for has some ideas. Then as the wishes are filled, the customer service department will let you know, and you'll pack things up and deliver them.''

Zack shrugged. "You're right. It sounds pretty easy."

"I said *simple*, not *easy*. There are always snags. Gifts don't come in at a nice, steady pace, and sometimes one member of a family is passed over altogether. There's a fund provided by the store, so you can go shopping to fill in all the gaps.''

Zack didn't look enthusiastic at the prospect.

The longer Brandi thought about it, though, the happier she was that he'd taken over the Wishing Tree. If he gave the project the attention it needed, he wouldn't have time to annoy her. "Just think," she consoled him, "all that time you've spent wandering around the store looking at the merchandise won't be wasted after all. I'm sure *somebody* would like that steamer you bought for your sister.''

The manicotti was perfectly cooked but literally too hot to eat, so they dawdled over dinner, and it was mid-evening before they got back to the mall. "Are you going into the store or home?" Zack asked.

Brandi yawned. "Home, I think. After a couple of glasses of wine I probably wouldn't get much done in the office anyway.''

Zack eyed her in mock disappointment. "I'm shocked at you, Ms. Ogilvie. *I* have to go back to work. And you were late this morning, too. Maybe I should report you to Ross.''

"Go ahead. You'll no doubt find him at home.''

Zack parked his car next to hers. "Meaning that he doesn't work sixteen-hour days? That's a good question, you know. If the CEO doesn't have to, why do you?"

"Because he's the CEO, and I'm not. He's already at the top and I'm still climbing. Sit still, Zack—don't bother to come around and help me out."

Her protest came too late, though; he was already out of the car. She'd parked in the farthest corner again, and the lights were dimmer here. Zack seemed to loom over her as he had last night—right before he'd kissed her. He was awfully close. Brandi wondered if he was thinking of doing it again, and told herself that the odd little ripple in her nerves was anxiety.

"Thanks for dinner," she said quickly, as she slipped her key into the door lock. "I still think you should have let me pay for it, though, since it was store business."

"That's okay. You can take me out for lobster someday, and I promise not to protest." But he smiled as he said it.

She couldn't close her door because he was standing in the way, almost leaning over her as if he was inspecting the equipment—or her. "And you said *my* car's nice," he murmured.

Brandi almost laughed in relief. "If you think I'm going to get into that argument, you're crazy." She turned the key in the ignition. The only sound was an ominous clicking from somewhere in the engine. "What the—" She tried again.

"Your battery's dead, so you might as well give it up." Zack put a fingertip on the switch that controlled the headlights and gently pushed; the switch clicked off.

Brandi groaned. "The sun was just coming up when I got to work this morning, and I must have left the lights on. What an idiotic thing to do!"

"No, it's not. But why don't you use the setting that automatically turns the headlights off?"

"Because I don't trust it to work," she admitted.

Zack didn't laugh; she gave him credit for that. But even in the dim glow of the parking-lot lights, she could see the gleam of humor in his eyes.

"All right," she said irritably, "so I'm a fool, too."

"I didn't say that, Brandi."

"Well, you don't have to stick around. Though I would appreciate it if you'd pull out your magic little telephone and call a wrecker for me."

Zack shook his head. "I would, but—"

"I know, you've used up all your free time."

"It wouldn't do any good to jump-start the engine unless you plan to drive around for an hour or two to recharge the battery. Otherwise, it'll be dead again by morning."

"Oh. I hadn't thought of that."

"Besides, do you really want to sit here in the cold and wait? The wrecker guys are probably hours behind on their calls, with the snow. You'd be better off to leave it till tomorrow."

Brandi had to admit he was right. "In that case, Santa's Friend, how about doing your good deed for the day?"

"And take you home? I'd love to, but I'm supposed to go on duty in fifteen minutes, and I'm afraid if I don't turn up for my last half hour of work the boss will fire me."

"Zack—" She waved a hand at the thinly populated parking lot. "Skip it. Nobody's there anyway."

"Certainly. But may I have that in writing?" Brandi stuck her tongue out at him. Zack grinned and helped her into his car again. "Did you lock your car?" he asked.

"You think someone's going to hot-wire that vehicle and drive it off if I didn't? Of course I did, Zack—I've lived in this city all my life. I always lock doors."

"And turn off headlights?" But the smile that tugged at the corner of his mouth made it a teasing comment, not a tormenting one, and Brandi was surprised to find herself feeling almost warm because of it. Warm, and a little confused. What was happening to her anyway?

She gave him directions to her apartment complex, and when they arrived she unfastened her seat belt and let him help her out of the car. "Would you like a cup of coffee, Zack? Nothing fancy—I haven't been to the supermarket in days—but..."

It was the least she could do. He'd bailed her out of a jam after all. It was only friendly to offer him a hot drink. He'd probably turn her down anyway; he'd be anxious to get home, too.

Zack smiled and said, "I'd like that."

Brandi swallowed hard. It wasn't fair, she thought. All the man had done was smile, and the odd, breathless ache she'd felt this morning—when she'd been assaulted by that sudden, idiotic urge to kiss the dimple in his cheek—swept over her once more.

She found herself wondering what he'd have done if she actually acted on that kooky impulse. Not that she had any intention of finding out, she assured herself. A cup of coffee, a little polite conversation, and he'd be out the door.

Just outside her apartment was a visitor, obviously waiting for the bell to be answered. As they approached, the girl swung around to face them, and Brandi recognized her as one of the three who had been selling garlands the night before. Her arms were full of evergreens.

"Oh, you're finally home," she said with obvious relief. "I've got your garland, you see."

Brandi frowned. "I thought I told you to give it to someone who wanted it."

"But I can't. My mother got really annoyed with me, and said I couldn't sell things to people and then not deliver them. So here." She thrust the sharp-scented greenery into Brandi's arms and hurried away.

"Well, isn't that a switch," Brandi muttered. "All I tried to do was make a donation, and now I'm stuck with this thing." The bundle was huge and prickly; she shifted it gingerly and tried to reach her key. "And I do mean *stuck*. Do you want a garland?"

"No, but I'll hold it for you." Zack rescued her from the evergreens. "Can't you use it?"

"I don't decorate for Christmas."

"Not at all? Don't you celebrate it, either?"

"Of course I celebrate, in my own style. I'll collapse and rest up from the rush and get recharged for the next one—the after-Christmas sales and returns."

Zack frowned. "That doesn't sound like much of a celebration. Don't you have a family?"

"Not really. My mother died when I was eighteen."

"That's a tough time to lose a parent."

She nodded curtly and went on. "My dad's in California. They divorced when I was little, and he's got a second family."

"So you don't feel you fit in?" Zack's tone was gentle.

His conclusion was true, but Brandi didn't feel like admitting it. The last thing she needed was well-meaning sympathy. "It's got nothing to do with that. I can't go dashing off halfway across the country in the midst of my busiest season for the sake of carving up a turkey."

"So you stay home and have a bologna sandwich by yourself."

"Something like that." She wasn't about to get drawn into a discussion of her habits. "Just dump the garland anywhere."

"What are you going to do with it?"

"I'll put it out with the garbage if I can't find anyone who wants it. Maybe some of your Wishing Tree people would like to have it. Coffee or hot chocolate? I think I have some of that powdered mix."

"Coffee's fine." He was still standing in the center of her living room, the garland in his arms, looking around. "It's a shame, you know. You've got a perfect place for a tree, right by the balcony doors so the neighbors can enjoy it, too."

He had to raise his voice, since Brandi had gone on to the kitchen. She put the kettle on and called back, "That's it, you see. On the rare occasions I'm in the mood to look at a Christmas tree, I just step onto the balcony and enjoy everyone else's. No fuss, no muss, no dropped needles . . ."

Zack didn't answer, and Brandi busied herself finding a tray—since she didn't entertain often, she had to look for it—and setting it up. "I don't have any fresh cream," she warned.

"I don't use it, remember? You know what you need to get you into the Christmas spirit? A couple of kids."

Brandi choked. "Oh, no. Never." She stepped around the corner and almost dropped the tray. Most of the garland was now draped neatly over the mantel; Zack was arranging the last few feet. And the gas log in the fireplace was burning brightly. "Make yourself at home," she said dryly.

"Thanks. Why no kids?"

"They're altogether too much responsibility."

Zack tipped his head to one side. "Were you a difficult kid?"

Brandi was puzzled at the question. "No more than most, I suppose. But it's a different world these days. People who aren't willing to be at home with their kids shouldn't have them in the first place."

"And you aren't willing?"

"Not particularly. I could hardly quit—I have enough to do making a living for myself as it is, without taking on a couple of people who'd need college educations one day. Besides, I told you I love my job."

"To say nothing of your ambitions for the future."

"That's right. Zack, the garland's kind of cute, but—"

He hadn't paused as they talked, and the last bit of greenery seemed to nestle down around the mantel as if it belonged there. "Doesn't that give the whole place a festive air?" He came to take the tray out of her hands and set it on the wicker trunk in front of the couch. "I didn't mean permanent kids anyway."

"You mean I could be sort of an adopted aunt to someone else's? I don't know any kids all that well. Besides, I don't seem to have the knack for getting along with them, and it's dead sure I don't have the time to learn it, even if I wanted to."

Zack didn't answer. He sat quietly, cradling his coffee cup in one hand, staring at the fire.

Brandi wondered what he was thinking, and the suspicion she'd felt earlier in the evening stirred to life again. But this time, as if her subconscious mind had spent the intervening time chewing on the problem, it was not just a half-formed hunch but much more.

She'd asked if he was a spy, and without pausing to consider, Zack had made a joke about Ross. Was it her imagination, or had there been something almost Freudian about how fast that answer had come? Did it mean he was working not for some rival of Tyler-Royale's, but for Ross Clayton himself?

He'd even had that very private telephone number, she reminded herself.

Brandi stirred sugar into her coffee and leaned back in her corner of the couch. "Ross has always had a troubleshooter he can call on," she said almost dreamily. "Someone who can go into any of the stores and diagnose and fix problems."

Zack's eyebrows rose. "What brought that up, Brandi?"

She didn't answer the question. "A few years back it was Whitney Townsend, but now she's settled in Kansas City. At the moment there doesn't seem to be a troubleshooter, because when San Antonio got into some minor difficulty a few weeks ago, Whitney went down to sort it out."

"I don't quite—"

"Or maybe there is a troubleshooter—but for some reason Ross doesn't want anyone to know just now who's doing the job. So he sent Whitney to take care of the small problem, and held the real troubleshooter in reserve for the big one."

Zack shrugged as if he was willing to humor her by playing along. "Secrecy could be an advantage for Ross at times, I'm sure."

"Exactly." Her fingers were trembling. "And that's what made me start to wonder tonight about what you're really doing here. You're certainly not an ordinary Santa, Zack, so what are you? Are you Ross's troubleshooter? And if that *is* what's going on—then why are you here? What's wrong with my store? And why didn't I realize there was a problem before the head office did?"

CHAPTER SIX

THEN Brandi held her breath. Was her suspicion the truth? Was the trouble Ross had spoken of that first day not Zack's personal problem at all, but something wrong with the store?

And if it was, would Zack admit it?

The suspicion had been building in her mind all evening, and so quietly that Brandi had been unable to put her finger on it. Her misgivings had started when he'd showed her to his car—or maybe long before that, when she'd first noticed the quality of his Santa suit—and had finally burst forth in full flower.

The trouble was, even though the theory was her own, Brandi couldn't quite make herself believe she'd hit on the right answer. She couldn't imagine how she could be oblivious to a problem large enough to cause that kind of response; even now, she couldn't begin to think of anything going on in the store that would upset anyone in the head office.

But there was something strange going on—and she could find no other combination of circumstances that made sense. Zack's explanation of why he was still using his cellular phone despite a financial downturn might hold water—but the easy dismissal of his expensive car didn't.

"You may have to run that one past me again." Zack sounded as if she'd hit him solidly right in the diaphragm.

As if he was startled, Brandi thought. But was he surprised at the accusation because it was false, or because he'd been discovered?

He went on, "Ross wouldn't go behind your back like that, would he?"

"He has before," Brandi said. "Not with me, exactly. I mean other managers, in other circumstances. Whitney Townsend's told me some tales about investigating a store without telling the manager."

"How could you be unaware of a problem so bad that Ross would go into overdrive about it?"

Brandi's eyelids were stinging. She shut her eyes to try to keep the tears from showing. She was a professional woman, and she didn't cry about business matters; what had come over her anyway? "I don't know," she mumbled. "I don't know."

The silence was oppressive.

Zack hadn't really answered her question, she realized, and she found herself wishing that she hadn't said anything at all. If it was true, she wasn't helping the situation by blubbering about it like a baby. And if it wasn't true, she'd simply made a fool of herself.

Zack slid closer. She could feel the warmth of his body next to her even before he slipped a hand under her chin and raised her face to his. "Brandi, look at me."

She had to make a great effort to open her eyes.

Zack's voice was husky. "Nothing like that is going on. The troubles I'm dealing with are my own."

Her unshed tears made his face look blurry, but despite that fact, Brandi thought he had never looked better. "You're telling the truth, Zack?" she whispered.

"I swear it. From everything I can see, the store is doing beautifully, and you..." He paused, and said something under his breath that Brandi didn't quite catch. Then he bent his head to very deliberately kiss a tear from her eyelashes. "And you are beautiful, too," he whispered, and his mouth claimed hers.

Already emotionally off balance because of her fears, Brandi reacted to his kiss almost as she would have if she'd stepped off a cliff. She was dizzy, and her stomach had an all-gone feeling as if she'd looked down and found nothing but air beneath her feet. Her breath came in painful gasps, and she clutched at Zack.

He eased her back against the couch, but that didn't seem to help, for each kiss increased her dizziness. The only thing she could depend on was the strength of Zack's arms holding her, cradling her, keeping her safe. He was the one remaining solid object in a world gone suddenly topsy-turvy, and so she pressed against him and kissed him back, until suddenly she didn't care if she fell all the way to the center of the earth, so long as he was with her. Her ears were ringing already—had she fallen so far?—but she hardly noticed.

Zack pulled back a little. Brandi murmured a protest and tried to draw him down into her arms once more, but he resisted.

Brandi frowned a bit. Her senses came flooding back, and she realized the telephone was ringing. How had she gotten so frazzled that she hadn't even heard it? And what did Zack think of her preoccupation—for obviously *he* hadn't been so carried away that he'd missed it.

She was still a little light-headed, and she had to clutch at the door frame to steady herself as she went into the kitchen to answer the phone.

She recognized the voice; it belonged to one of the security guards at the store, and he sounded tense. "Ms. Ogilvie? There's been a little trouble down here. It's over now, but I thought I should call you anyway."

Brandi shook off her giddy feeling. "What happened?" Midway through the guard's explanation, she cut him off. "I'll be there as soon as I can."

Zack was standing in the center of the carpet when she came back into the living room. Had he heard the conversation, Brandi wondered, or was he on his feet because he intended to leave just as soon as possible?

While she wasn't naive enough to think Zack hadn't enjoyed that kiss, the whole situation *was* a little awkward. She'd kissed the man as if she was starving—as if she expected never to have another chance to be held and caressed. She wondered if he thought she'd thrown herself at him; she couldn't blame him if he did.

Her voice was a little tense. "I hate to ask for another favor, Zack, but can you take me back to the store?"

He reached for the coat he'd draped across the back of a chair. "Trouble?"

"Remember the weird guy the security guard warned us about?"

"You mean the one who was hanging around the parking lot last night?"

Brandi was momentarily distracted. Had it really only been last night that Zack had walked her to her car—and kissed her? She pushed the memory to the back of her mind. "Tonight he tried to hold up the clerk at the perfume counter just inside the main door from the mall. She reached for the panic button instead of the cash, and he gave her a shove and ran." She slid her arms into the coat he was holding for her. "I should have been there."

Zack gave her shoulders a sympathetic squeeze. "And just what do you think you'd have been able to do about it?"

"That's beside the point. It's my store, and my job." She flipped her hair over her coat collar, and the gleaming auburn mass hit him squarely in the face. "Sorry. I didn't mean to swat you with my hair."

Zack shook his head a little, as if the blow—light as it was—had stunned him. "A robbery—right in the mall?"

Brandi nodded. "Crazy, isn't it? He'd have to run a hundred yards down the mall to get outside."

"Or else cut across the store to the parking-lot exits."

"Yes—but either way, he might run into any number of security people before he got out of the building and away."

"Did they get him?"

"I guess not," Brandi said reluctantly. "By the time the clerk could stop screaming and tell anyone what had happened, the guy was long gone."

"Then maybe he wasn't so crazy after all."

Brandi settled into the passenger seat and nibbled at her thumbnail. "Fortunately the clerk wasn't badly hurt—just shook up and maybe bruised a bit. You know, I've always felt we were safe from that sort of thing, just because there are seventy stores and hundreds of people around all the time, and it would be so difficult for a robber to get away."

"Maybe this kook isn't smart enough to think about things like that."

Brandi shivered. "If you're trying to make me feel better, Zack, you're not getting the job done. I'd rather think a would-be robber would be smart enough to think through the consequences, because if he isn't, anything might happen." She lapsed into silence, which lasted till they arrived at the mall.

Closing time had passed, so Zack ignored the no-parking signs and pulled up in the fire lane beside the mall entrance nearest the Tyler-Royale store. Just a few yards away were three police cars, lights flashing.

"Zack," Brandi said slowly as they crossed the sidewalk to the mall entrance. "About what I said earlier—I'm sorry I accused you of being involved in some kind of plot.''

Zack silently held the door for her.

Brandi went on. ''I must have sounded absolutely paranoid. When something threatens this store, or even appears to... well, I go a little crazy, I'm afraid.''

''Brandi—''

The tone of his voice scared her; he sounded almost somber. Brandi hoped he didn't intend to discuss the kiss they'd shared, and how it fit into the pattern of her behavior. She couldn't look straight at him. ''This isn't the time or the place for a chat, Zack. So can we just forget it happened? Please?'' She didn't wait for an answer.

Inside the Tyler-Royale store, a knot of people was gathered around the perfume and cosmetics counter nearest the atrium entrance. The still-shaken employee was sitting on a tall stool, twisting a handkerchief in her fingers and talking to two policemen. She didn't even see Brandi.

The security guard came hurrying up. ''I'm sorry if I woke you, Ms. Ogilvie, but I thought—''

''You didn't, John. I'm glad you called.''

''Oh? You sure sounded funny, like you'd just dozed off.'' The man glanced from her to Zack, who was standing just a step behind her, and suddenly a tinge of red appeared in his face.

Obviously, Brandi thought, he'd gotten the wrong idea. There was no point in trying to correct his impression, though; any kind of protest would sound fishy. She said crisply, ''Where's the Doberman?''

''In his kennel. I thought with all the cops around, we didn't need the confusion of a dog just now.''

''You're sure you won't need him?''

The guard nodded. "The guy's long gone. Lots of people saw him go, but they didn't realize what was happening in time to stop him."

"Of course." Brandi turned to Zack. "This is obviously going to take a while. You don't need to wait around."

"How would you get home if I left?"

"Someone will give me a ride. Or I'll take a cab."

The perfume clerk heard her and turned around. She looked pale and shaken, and when Brandi patted her shoulder, she burst into tears.

Brandi put both arms around the woman. "It's all right," she whispered. "You did just fine."

"But Ms. Ogilvie," the woman wailed, "the policeman says I should just have given the robber the money!"

Brandi shot a look of acute dislike at the nearest cop. No doubt he was right; no amount of money was worth the risk of a life. But now was hardly the time to suggest to a shaken woman that she'd done precisely the wrong thing. "Well, it's done now," Brandi said soothingly. "And you did the very best you could. When you're finished with the interviews, we'll make sure you get home, and you can take as much time off as you need."

The policeman said gruffly, "I'm finished. She should probably be checked out at a hospital, though." After the employee had gone, leaning on a co-worker's arm, he turned back to Brandi and folded his arms across his chest. "Worried about the money, are you? Well, he didn't get any, so I guess in your view she handled it exactly right."

"Of course she didn't," Brandi snapped. "But did you really think you'd make her sleep better tonight by pointing out she could have gotten killed because of the way she handled it?"

Zack moved a little closer. "Brandi..."

Brandi bit her lip. She didn't look at Zack, but at the policeman. "I'm sorry. Look, if you want to come back and teach all my employees the proper response, I'd be glad to have you. But scaring her a little more tonight isn't going to help anything."

She thought she saw, from the corner of her eye, a smile tugging at Zack's lips.

The police looked for another half hour to be certain the would-be robber hadn't left any fingerprints or dropped any belongings, but finally they finished up, and Brandi was free to go. The store was quiet by then. She could hear the soft click of the Doberman's toenails against the hard-surfaced floors as the guard made his regular rounds. Brandi yawned as she said good-night, and wondered how long it would take for a cab to show up.

But Zack hadn't gone after all. He was sitting quietly on a carpeted display cube at the far side of the atrium, and when Brandi came toward him he stood up and slid a hand under her elbow.

The warm support was welcome, but Brandi wasn't in the mood to talk. Zack seemed content with the silence, as well. It wasn't until they were almost back at her apartment complex that he said, "You're a thoroughly confusing creature, Brandi."

She was puzzled. "I don't know what you mean."

Zack didn't answer. Instead he said, "You'll be all right alone?"

It didn't sound like a question, but a statement. Obviously, Brandi thought, whether she'd invited him or not, he didn't intend to come in. Well, that was all right with her; it was late, and she was drained.

Still, she couldn't help but wonder what his reasons were. Was he simply tired himself? It would be no wonder; he'd had a long day, too. Was he being sensitive to her exhaustion? Or was he still wary of what had happened between them earlier this evening?

"I'll be fine," she said. "After all, I'm not the one who got held up."

He parked the car and helped her out. "You don't depend on anybody but yourself, do you, Brandi?"

She shrugged. "Who else am I supposed to depend on?"

He didn't answer that, and he didn't make any other move to touch her. He leaned against the passenger door and watched till she was safely inside the building.

Despite the central heating in her apartment, Brandi felt cold. That was the aftermath of shock, no doubt, from the evening's events. Tyler-Royale had its share of shoplifters. The main office had discovered an embezzler once, and now and then a store was burglarized. But so far as Brandi knew, this was the first time any of the stores had actually been robbed during business hours.

It was no wonder she was still feeling stunned. But was the robbery the only reason she was upset? Was she still suffering the aftereffects of that kiss, as well? Things had come very close to getting out of control. What would have happened if the security guard hadn't interrupted?

Nothing, she told herself. She certainly knew better than to allow it.

She warmed her hands over the fireplace. She'd been in such a hurry to get to the store that neither of them had remembered to turn the gas log off. Fortunately Zack had put the fire screen in place, so there had been no danger.

The sharp scent of evergreen seemed to float from the garland atop the mantel and fill the room. Zack had done a good job of arranging it; nevertheless the greenery was a little bare. Brandi knew exactly what would make it look right—some twinkling lights twisted through the branches and a scattering of small, bright-colored ornaments. Then the barest dusting of spray snow on the end of the needles, with some glitter for emphasis, and the garland would be perfect.

Not that she would do any of those things. There wasn't any point to it when she was scarcely ever home.

Zack had said this evening that she needed a couple of kids to get her into the Christmas spirit. Well, she didn't know about getting into the spirit—it seemed to her that having a couple of little people around for the holidays was likely to do nothing but increase her level of exhaustion.

The mental image she'd created in Toyland this evening, as she watched Zack playing with the kids and the train, sprang unbidden to her mind once more. In fact, if she closed her eyes halfway she could almost *see* that scene. A decorated tree stood beside the patio doors where he'd said it should go, and the train went round and round the track as two children in fuzzy sleepers knelt to watch. She couldn't see their faces, but they weren't very old.

Once, she had assumed she'd have children one day. It wasn't something she'd thought a great deal about; she'd never been around children much, and she had no great longing for them. But kids were part of the package of life—when the time was right, there would be a man and a marriage, and ultimately, a family.

And up to a point, things had followed the pattern. There had been a man; there had very nearly been a marriage. Thank heaven, she thought, that it hadn't come to that, for Jason didn't really want a wife, he wanted a caretaker.

Zack had observed tonight that she depended only on herself. Brandi could have told him, if she'd wanted to, how she'd learned that lesson not once but over and over. First from her father, who'd seldom shown interest in her after the divorce. Then her mother had died, and—unfair though it was to blame her for that—Brandi had felt abandoned once more. And, finally and most cruelly, there was Jason, who said he admired her independence, but meant only that he appreciated the freedom it offered him to be untroubled and irresponsible.

But she hadn't told Zack any of that, and she wouldn't. Sharing so much with someone she barely knew would be asking for another kind of hurt, and Brandi had learned the hard way not to allow herself that kind of weakness. She didn't need anyone to confide in anyway. She was used to depending only on herself. That she knew how to do.

The apartment was so quiet she could hear her own heartbeat. So quiet that she was tempted to talk to herself just to hear a voice.

Maybe she should get a cat to keep her company. Talking to an animal was nothing like talking to herself. Nobody would think she was crazy if she talked to a pet.

And having a cat around would certainly be less troublesome than dealing with a man. Particularly, she thought, with her sense of humor restored, a man like Zack Forrest!

Brandi was running late. Saturdays were always busy at the store, and this afternoon she'd had to deal with a series of unhappy customers who wanted to talk to the manager. Then the personnel manager had come in to complain that Zack was sending half his Wishing Tree clients upstairs to apply for jobs. And after that, she'd stopped to visit the perfume clerk to see how she was getting along after the robbery attempt.

As a result, Brandi was still feeling a little frazzled when she turned her car over to the valet in front of Ross Clayton's lakeshore mansion, and her palms were just a little damp as she started up the long walk to the immense carved front door.

Under the circumstances, she'd rather be almost any-where than here tonight. If it wasn't for Whitney Townsend's order to attend, she'd probably have found a last-minute excuse.

Brandi had never been particularly fond of business events that masqueraded as parties. It seemed such a waste of time to get dressed up to go out with the same people one saw regularly through the course of the job. If people were going to talk about their work anyway, she thought, why not just put them in a boardroom and let them get on with it? And if they weren't going to talk business, why were they bothering to get together in the first place? The only thing all these people had in common was Tyler-Royale.

No—*most* of these people had only the stores in common, she corrected herself. There was Zack, of course, and whatever other friends the Claytons had de-cided to include tonight to liven things up. Though even Zack had ties to the store...

Suspicion flickered once more at the back of her mind, and resolutely Brandi extinguished it. He had reassured her that her store was in no danger, and she had no reason to disbelieve him.

She might not even see Zack tonight anyway. She'd be busy with Whitney Townsend. Besides, there were so many Tyler-Royale executives that it was quite possible to circulate all evening and still not see every single one of them.

Every leaded-glass window in the Claytons' Tudor Revival mansion was aglow. Standing guard at each side of the walk were huge evergreens, crusted with snow and golden lights, which were reflected from the snow-covered grass.

Before Brandi reached the house, another car pulled up; she recognized the manager of the San Francisco store and paused on the sidewalk to let him and his wife catch up. She'd done part of her training in the San Francisco store, but she hadn't seen much of the couple since.

The night was cold and still; her breath hung in a cloud, and the manager's wife scolded her for waiting outside.

Brandi smiled and kissed her cheek. "I'm used to this kind of weather. And I wanted to say hello before we got into the crush inside." It was true; the fact that she didn't particularly want to walk into the party alone had little to do with it.

Why should she be feeling sensitive about that anyway? Certainly the crowd wasn't going to pause and hush to admire her new black velvet dress. All the Tyler-Royale people were used to Brandi appearing by herself; they'd hardly even notice.

But Zack would. And even though she'd told the truth about having a date, if he saw her coming in alone, he'd have good reason to wonder.

Not that he'd be looking, she reminded herself. So it was silly to go to any extra effort for his sake.

Just inside the massive carved oak front door, Ross Clayton and his wife were greeting their guests. Brandi hung back to let the San Francisco couple go ahead of her, but within a minute Ross took Brandi's hand and murmured, "Now who wins the honors for getting you to show up here tonight, I wonder?"

Brandi let her eyes widen just a little. "What on earth do you mean? Ross, you know I'd never miss a Tyler-Royale event unless I had overwhelming reason."

Ross chuckled. "I know. It's just our bad luck that you always seem to have overwhelming reason. Why not this time, that's what I'd like to know. Which reminds me, you've been awfully quiet all the way around for the past couple of days. How are things in Oak Park?"

Brandi shrugged. "Hectic, but what else is new? Have you ever considered moving the company Christmas parties to July? It would be a whole lot easier to fit them into everyone's schedules."

"You mean you'd actually like to fit them into yours? You amaze me."

Brandi bit her lip.

He smiled a little. "It's not a bad idea, actually. I'll consider it. You know, Brandi, that's one of your strengths. You always have a different way of looking at things."

"Thanks," Brandi said crisply. "At least I think that was a compliment."

Ross laughed. "Is Zack still working out so well?"

Brandi's eyes came to rest on the velvet lapel of Ross Clayton's tuxedo, where one of Zack's buttons proclaimed that he was Santa's Friend. "Depends. Do you want reassurance, or the truth?"

"Ouch. Maybe we should talk—"

Ross's wife interrupted. "Don't you think that's enough business, darling? You did promise me you'd lay off tonight and let everyone have a good time." She offered her cheek to Brandi. "We're using the guest room at the top of the stairs for the ladies' coats. The maid will take yours up if you'd like."

The San Francisco couple had already handed over their coats and moved off into the throng, and the guests who had followed Brandi in showed every sign of monopolizing Ross for the next ten minutes at least.

"Thanks," Brandi said, "but I'll go and comb my hair, too." That way, when she came back down, it wouldn't be like walking into the party alone. It was silly, she knew—all her life she'd been walking into parties by herself, so why should it bother her tonight?

She slowly climbed the massive staircase. From one of the lower steps, she had a good view of the big formal living room, and she paused to look over the crowd. She told herself she was trying to spot Whitney, but she was terribly aware that there was no sign of Zack, either. That should be no surprise, she decided; there were more guests here tonight than Brandi had seen at any other Tyler-Royale party she'd ever attended.

There were several women in the guest room, chatting as they fussed with their makeup, and the air was heavy with cologne and hair spray. Brandi laid her coat on the bed, ran a quick comb through her auburn curls, and left. It was better to take the chance of being considered rude then to risk a full-fledged sneezing fit by sticking around for another minute.

But even such a short stay in the overfragrant room had made her eyes water, and Brandi paused in a little alcove in the hallway, leaning against the paneling and trying to blot the moisture away with the edge of a lace-trimmed handkerchief.

Party noises drifted up the open stairs. From the room she'd just left came a woman's voice and an answering laugh. And from down the hall came a peal of childish giggles.

The Claytons' kids, she thought. No doubt their parents thought they were safety tucked away for the night. Brandi took a step toward the sound and then stopped; it was none of her business after all. Probably the children were with a sitter or a nanny anyway. She didn't know much about kids, but surely these were too young to be left on their own with their parents so busy.

A door opened, sending light streaming into the dimly lit hallway, and a small girl, perhaps three years old, appeared. She was holding the hem of her pink flannel nightgown up with both hands, and her chubby knees pumped as she ran down the hallway toward Brandi.

A man followed. The dim lights and the moisture in Brandi's eyes prevented her from seeing him clearly, but he looked incredibly tall compared to the child, and one of his steps corresponded to half a dozen of hers. Before the little girl had covered more than a couple of yards, he'd caught up with her, bent, and tossed her over one shoulder.

The child squealed happily.

"Shush, Kathleen," the man said, "or we'll have your mother up here and nobody will have any more fun."

His voice was rich and warm, and—despite the warning—loaded with good humor. At least, Brandi thought, this little scene explained why Ross had thought Zack would make a good Santa Claus.

She stepped out of the shadowed alcove. "Hello, Zack. Having a bit of trouble?"

"You might say," he answered. "The little varmint gave my bow tie a good yank and then ran."

Brandi took a good look at him. His dark trousers looked just a little rumpled, he wore no jacket over his stiffly pleated formal white shirt, and the ends of his tie dangled loose. She thought he looked wonderful.

The child giggled and grabbed for the tie again. "I got you, Uncle Zack! Didn't I?"

Uncle Zack? He'd mentioned a sister. Was it possible she was Ross Clayton's wife? And how did that all fit together?

"And now I've got you, nuisance." Zack shifted the child to a more comfortable position.

"Uncle Zack?" Brandi asked. "I didn't know you were related."

"I'm not—it's purely an honorary title." He studied Brandi's face. "Is something wrong?"

"No. Why?"

"You look as if you've been crying."

"Oh." She shook her head and tucked her handkerchief into her tiny black evening bag. "It's just all the scents in the cloakroom. I have to be careful at the store, as well. Too much perfume in the air and I'm a mess."

"That's good. I thought it might be something serious."

The child squirmed to get down, and effortlessly Zack rotated the little body into a firmer hold so she couldn't escape.

"You're obviously no amateur at this sort of thing," Brandi said. "Though I must say you don't look like a baby-sitter."

"Oh, after you turned me down for the party I figured I might as well be useful. These affairs are so deadly dull. Come and join us if you like."

His words were casual, but the way he looked at Brandi was anything but. Ever so slowly, his gaze roved over her, from the loose cloud of auburn curls, over the sleek black velvet of her dress to her high-heeled pumps, and back to her face again.

Brandi felt herself growing warm, and she had to force herself to stand still. He had warned her the day they met, she remembered, that sometime he'd give her a good looking-over. She supposed this was it.

"We were halfway through a game when Kathleen attacked me," Zack went on, "so I'd better finish or I'll have a mutiny from her big brother. Coming?"

Brandi hesitated. "I don't think so. I don't know anything about kids."

He smiled a little. "How do you think people learn?"

"Anyway," Brandi remembered with relief, "someone's waiting for me."

Zack's gaze skimmed her body once more. "Yes," he mused. "And getting impatient, no doubt. I can understand why they would be."

His voice was very slightly husky, and its effect on Brandi was like silk rubbing softly against her skin, creating an electrical charge that fluttered her pulse and did funny things to her breathing.

She retreated toward the stairs, trying her best to look dignified. She wasn't sure she succeeded.

CHAPTER SEVEN

BRANDI reached the bottom of the stairs before she realized she hadn't even been looking for Whitney. Instead, she'd been basking in the memory of Zack with the little girl in his arms.

The child had been charming. And Zack hadn't exactly been hard on the eyes, either, Brandi had to admit. Despite his slightly rumpled appearance—or perhaps because of it—he had a personal magnetism that she'd bet few of the other men at this party did. Zack looked better in half a tuxedo than most men did in the whole thing, and there was something heartwarming about a guy who ignored his dress-up clothes in order to play with a couple of kids—

Brandi shook her head in rueful disbelief. What was happening to her, for heaven's sake? She was suddenly discovering a romantic streak she'd never dreamed she possessed! What was it about kids anyway? It wasn't that she had anything against them—in fact, she'd hardly been around any kids since her own childhood days— but she'd never been one to coo over babies or be charmed by tiny tots. So why should she suddenly find Zack's Father Goose act appealing?

She tried to focus her attention on the swirl of guests. Surely by now Whitney would be here, and once busy with her friend, Brandi would forget all about Zack.

The party had grown even larger in the few minutes Brandi had been upstairs. More guests were streaming in, and she had trouble making her way through the entrance hall and into the living room. Standing near the enormous, glittering Christmas tree in a bay window was a group of executives; they waved her over, but Brandi smiled and shook her head, and went on looking for Whitney.

The massive doors between the main rooms had been thrown open, and waiters were circulating with trays of drinks and hors d'oeuvres. Brandi took a glass of champagne and wandered toward the dining room.

But her progress was slow; several times she was interrupted by people who exclaimed over how well she looked and how long it had been since they'd seen her. They made such a big deal of it that Brandi began to feel guilty. Just how long *had* it been since she'd attended one of these parties anyway?

She'd just spotted Whitney, at the far side of the dining room, when the manager of the Minneapolis store buttonholed her to ask how she was planning to handle the new bookkeeping system that the head office was putting into place. It took twenty minutes to dislodge him, and by then the cocktail hour was over and people were starting to drift out of the room.

Brandi was just looking around for her friend again when Whitney appeared beside her, tall and sleek in pure white silk and a neckline that outdid every other woman in the room.

"*There* you are," Whitney announced with relief. "I was beginning to think you'd stood me up after all."

"I wouldn't dare," Brandi admitted, and gave her a hug. "You look wonderful!"

The man beside Whitney gave a little snort. Whitney turned to him with a stunning smile. "You've already made it clear what you think of the neckline, Max, so no further editorial comment is necessary. You remember Max, don't you, Brandi?"

"Of course." Brandi extended a hand to Whitney's husband.

Whitney glanced around the room. "I suppose we'd better move toward the pool—that's where dinner is being served." She eyed Brandi. "It's very polite of you not to wrinkle your nose. When I first heard about it, I couldn't help telling Ross he had to be kidding."

"Well...it is a beautiful pool. But—"

"Not anymore. His newest innovation is a portable dance floor that sort of hangs over the water. Can you imagine?" But Whitney seemed only half-interested; her gaze was moving steadily across the room. "Drat the man, where *is* he? I saw him just a minute ago."

"You mean Ross? He was in the front hall when I came down from the cloakroom, but that was at least half an hour ago."

"Why would I want Ross?"

Brandi's heart gave an odd little leap. "Then who are you searching for?"

Whitney said sweetly, "Don't look at me like that, darling. I'm not matchmaking."

"Of course you're not. You've got far better sense than that." But Brandi's breath was doing odd little things, nevertheless.

"Not that I wouldn't, if I thought it might do some good," Whitney admitted. "But in this case I'm completely innocent. The new manager of the Seattle store is here, and it's his first corporate party, so I thought it would be nice to make him feel at home."

It wasn't Zack, then. And come to think of it, why should Brandi have jumped to the conclusion that he was the one Whitney meant? Zack could hardly be the only unattached male in a crowd like this. Who was to say Whitney even knew him? In fact, Brandi was sure she'd mentioned Whitney's name the other night, and Zack hadn't reacted at all.

None of which explained the twinge of disappointment she felt—which of course was an utterly ridiculous reaction. "It's sweet of you to look out for him."

"So's he," Whitney murmured. "Sweet, I mean. Not that I'd expect you to notice that on your own. We may as well go on. He'll catch up with us sooner or later, as the seating's all arranged."

The pool occupied a much newer wing of the house. The high-arched ceiling and glass walls allowed the space to act as a conservatory, as well, and huge green plants softened the sharp angles and hard surfaces. Tonight, since the snow-covered lawns outside were lit as brightly as the interior, the glass almost vanished and the pool wing seemed to be an island of tropical warmth floating freely in a sea of winter.

Tables for four were set up all around the perimeter of the room, and a band's equipment was ready in a corner. It took a close eye to recognize the pool in the center of the room, covered as it was by a hardwood dance floor, elevated a step above the surrounding area.

"It looks pretty solid," Brandi said.

"Well, that's one thing in its favor," Whitney murmured. "If it hadn't, I wouldn't have set foot on it."

A dark-clad arm slid around Whitney's waist, and she gave a little crow of surprise as Zack kissed her cheek.

Brandi was startled. Zack in half a tux had been impressive enough, but the complete picture was stunning. She'd known from the first time she met him that he looked wonderful in black, but she hadn't dreamed of this magnificence. He certainly didn't look as if he'd been roughhousing with a couple of children within the last hour.

He wasn't paying any attention to Brandi, but looked instead at Whitney as if she was the focus of all his dreams. "Lovely dress, dear," he said. "Of course, I'm surprised Max let you out of the house displaying that neckline."

"Watch what you say, Zack," Max warned. "Or you'll have a whole lot of guys laughing up their sleeves at you when your wife turns up wearing a dress like that."

There was a strange all-gone feeling in the pit of Brandi's stomach. A wife? But he'd asked her to come to this party with him!

Of course, no one had ever told her Zack *wasn't* married. And there was certainly no reason she should be feeling let down over it, Brandi told herself crossly.

"And I will happily help her choose it, too," Whitney said. "Though I'll no doubt be hobbling 'round the store with my walker by the time you get married."

The surge of relief that sang through Brandi's veins made her feel weak—and then angry. What was happening to her anyway?

"I'll take my chances," Zack murmured. "Our table is right at poolside." He smiled at Brandi and took her hand, holding it between his two. "Isn't that delightful?"

Our table? But hadn't Whitney said just a minute ago that the seating was prearranged? "Hold it," Brandi said. "*He's* the new manager in Seattle?"

Zack looked horrified. "Who told you that?"

"Of course he's not," Whitney said. "And he's not joining us for dinner, either. As a matter of fact, I'm not even going to introduce him to you. Look, Zack, just be a good boy and go away, will you?"

"You don't have to introduce us," Brandi said. "We've already met." The way he was looking at her made the room feel a little too warm all of a sudden.

He was still holding her hand, too, but Brandi noticed that fact only when he raised her fingers to his lips.

Whitney looked exasperated. "How?"

Zack said, "I make it a point to get acquainted with every pretty woman at a party." He drew Brandi toward the table and pulled out her chair.

"I know you do." Whitney's voice was dry. "And that's exactly why I wasn't planning to introduce you— I'm not about to give you my seal of approval. Brandi isn't simply a pretty woman at a party. She's worth three of you, Forrest. So go away, will you?"

Zack gave no indication that he'd even heard the order.

Brandi decided it was nice to know that it wasn't just her he ignored in order to do as he pleased. It was some relief to find that Zack could be as immovable as the Rock of Gibraltar where others were concerned, too.

He seated Brandi with a flourish and moved around the table to hold Whitney's chair, as well. Whitney glared at him; he simply pointed at the tiny name cards that adorned each place. She read them, and finally sighed and sat down. "Is there nothing you won't descend to, Zack?" she asked. "I thought rearranging place cards was too low even for you, but..."

He looked innocent. "I never touched them."

"Then you bribed somebody who did," Whitney muttered. "It's the same thing."

"Oh, you really wouldn't have liked the Seattle person. He's too agreeable—he'd have bored you stiff before you'd eaten your appetizer."

"Well, there's certainly no danger of that with you, is there?" Whitney said sweetly. "How did you two meet anyway?"

"Zack's the newest Santa at my store," Brandi said.

"*Zack*?" Whitney sounded horrified.

"Didn't Ross tell you?" Zack asked.

"Don't tell me it was his idea," Whitney said firmly.

Brandi murmured, "It certainly wasn't mine."

Max leaned forward. "We haven't had a chance to talk to Ross. We just got in a half hour before the party."

A uniformed waiter brought their appetizers, huge, succulent shrimp marinated in a vinaigrette dressing.

After the waiter was gone, Zack added thoughtfully, "Ross probably didn't mention it because he felt bad for me. This is just to tide me over some troubled times, you understand."

"No doubt you'll get back on your feet eventually," Whitney said.

"Oh, I'm sure of it."

"I can't wait to see this," Whitney said.

"What? Getting back on my feet, or playing Santa? You can catch the late performance tonight, if you like— I'm scheduled to work the last hour the store's open." Zack glanced at his watch. "You'll help me keep an eye on the time, won't you, Brandi?"

"That's a crazy schedule," Whitney said.

"I'm not complaining."

"You'd better not be," Brandi said softly, "because you chose it yourself."

"You were very firm about the idea of my setting my own hours."

"I also told you I was willing to negotiate that schedule, Zack."

He smiled. "Does that mean you'd rather I stayed here tonight instead of going back to the store? That's wonderful, Brandi, because it was going to make a terrible dent in the party for both of us if I had to leave."

Whitney looked as if the shrimp she'd just bitten into tasted sour, but she didn't say anything.

Brandi studied her with puzzlement. She'd known Whitney Townsend for several years, ever since Brandi

had started her management training course under
Whitney's supervision, but she'd never seen the woman
at a loss for words before.

"It's a fascinating job," Zack went on airily. "I'm
getting quite attached to it. There's no predicting it, you
see. One minute I'm getting smeared with chocolate-
covered kisses, and the next I'm defending the whole
idea of Santa Claus to a kid who's really too old to be
sitting on anyone's knee. Yesterday I not only rescued
a lost child, but I stanched a bloody nose after two kids
got in an argument about whose turn it was. I felt im-
mensely valuable."

Brandi frowned. "I didn't see a report on that."

"What? The bloody nose? It was no big deal. They
stopped the fight themselves as soon as they remembered Santa was watching."

"Anytime a customer needs medical attention, I
should be notified, Zack."

"The situation didn't require medical attention so
much as comfort. It was a very minor bloody nose."

"Still—"

"You know, Brandi, it wouldn't hurt if you'd learn
to delegate some authority."

Zack's tone was mild, but the reprimand stung a bit
anyway. Brandi was annoyed not only at the remark but
at her reaction to it—why should she be feeling sensitive
over his criticism? It was her store, and her responsibility, and he had no business criticizing her.

And he ought to have notified her; the policy
handbook he'd been given stated very clearly that any
time a customer needed medical attention, no matter how
minor the situation appeared, the matter was to be
brought to management's attention. Minor ailments
could become big ones, and the store could end up being

held responsible, especially if there was no proof of what had actually been done for the customer.

Didn't Zack understand that rules weren't simply made for the fun of it, but for good reason? Just a couple of days ago he'd agreed to consult her on important matters—but already he was taking things into his own hands again.

"Too bad it's such seasonal work," Whitney was saying. "You could make a career of it."

"That's a thought. Maybe I could play St. Valentine next, and then a leprechaun. And I'm sure there's an opening for the Easter Bunny. The costume might be a little uncomfortable, though—all that heavy fur."

The band had begun to play by the time they finished their appetizers, and Max leaned across to Brandi and asked her to dance. There was nothing Brandi wanted less right then, but good manners forbade her to refuse.

The music was slow and easy, and she could look over Max's shoulder and see the two at the table deep in conversation. "I wonder what they're talking about," she said finally.

"Probably not the Easter Bunny. Beyond that, I haven't a clue."

Ross Clayton appeared beside them. "May I cut in, Max?"

Brandi waited till Max was out of hearing, and said, "What kind of hold has Zack Forrest got on you, Ross?"

"You mean like blackmail material?" Ross was obviously amused. "Why? What's he been telling you?"

"Nothing much. That's part of the problem." Brandi stopped herself just in time; it wasn't exactly prudent to complain to the boss about a difficulty she ought to be able to solve herself. "How well do you know this guy, Ross?"

"Pretty well. Don't worry—he's a bit of a free spirit, but perfectly harmless."

Brandi looked up at him through narrowed eyes. "I'm charmed to hear it," she murmured, and wondered what her personnel director would have said about that. Sending the Wishing Tree clients upstairs for job interviews was another thing she'd have to bring up the next time she got a chance to talk to Mr. Free Spirit in private; he apparently thought he was running an employment agency. "He seems to be enjoying the Wishing Tree, at any rate."

"I think he'd like to be more involved," Ross went on.

"Oh, don't worry about that." Brandi's voice dripped irony. "He does just fine at minding other people's business."

Zack tapped Ross's shoulder. "Something tells me I'm being discussed," he murmured. "Ross, did Brandi tell you the manager of Toyland wants me to replace him when he retires after Christmas? No? I didn't think she would." He slid an arm around Brandi just as the music changed to a soft, slow, romantic beat, and drew her close.

"I didn't tell him because I didn't know it." Brandi missed a step, and Zack's arm tightened a little more.

She was feeling a little light-headed, but she wasn't sure if it was because of the intimate way he was holding her or the announcement he'd made. The idea of having Zack around on a more or less permanent basis was enough to make any store manager lose her grip, that was sure.

She lifted her chin. It was uncomfortable to look straight at him when he was holding her so close. "The only thing he's said to me is that you're running him off his feet with special orders for oddball toys."

"I know. He's extremely proud of me. The increased volume alone—"

"Oh, really? I thought he sounded plenty worried. It'll be wonderful if everything comes in, of course— but what if it doesn't, Zack? We're going to have a lot of unhappy parents and infuriated kids."

"So that means we shouldn't try? I didn't make promises, you know."

Brandi shook her head. "Sometimes it doesn't matter how carefully you say it, customers still think you've promised. Maybe I'll just put you in charge of complaints, and then you'll have to deal with the mess you've made."

"Do you always assume it's going to be a mess, Brandi?" His voice was easy, almost casual.

The question startled her a bit. "Of course not. The store would never get anywhere if I had that attitude. We'd never try anything new."

"So your hesitation only applies to me?"

"You must admit you're a bit more challenging than the average employee, Zack."

He didn't smile as she'd expected he would. A moment later, he said, "Can we leave business for another day and just enjoy the party?"

Brandi shrugged. "I'm enjoying myself as it is." She was a bit surprised to find that she was telling the exact truth, and also a little concerned that Zack might think she meant it was his presence that pleased her so much. "I mean—"

"Are you happy, Brandi?"

Happy? That was an odd question. "If you mean does the blood sing joyfully in my veins every single minute of my life, no. But I'm content. I like my job—"

"Is that all you want? All you need? Are you satisfied to be just content?"

"I have goals, of course," she said a bit stiffly. "But you said you didn't want to talk about business. What do you mean anyway? Not many people are all that wildly happy, you know. Simply being content isn't a bad thing at all."

"It's not enough for me. I want the world—all the wild swings and the breathless joy and the overwhelming ecstasy there is to be had."

Brandi shook her head. "Sounds uncomfortable."

"At least it's never boring."

"Just because something's consistent doesn't make it boring, Zack."

He was silent, as if he was thinking that over.

Brandi decided the conversation had gotten a bit too serious. Why was it that talking about happiness could be so depressing anyway? "By the way, what did you do to the man from Seattle?"

He smiled. "Nothing much. I simply introduced him to the sultry lady clothing buyer from Atlanta."

"Was that before or after you switched the place cards?"

"I'm wounded, Brandi. I didn't do that—he did."

"At your suggestion?"

"Well, I did tell him where everyone was sitting," Zack admitted. "Don't take it personally, though—she really is very attractive, and he hadn't caught so much as a glimpse of you at that point."

"I'm surprised, if she's such a stunner, that you didn't reserve her for yourself," Brandi said sweetly.

Zack slanted a look down at her and smiled, and Brandi's heart seemed to turn over. She couldn't look away, and for an instant, her body felt numb and completely out of her control. She stumbled, and Zack drew her closer still. She could feel his breath stirring the hair at her temple, and the warmth of his hand seemed to melt the black velvet at her waist. She wanted to stretch up on her toes and kiss that delightful dimple in his cheek, and then close her eyes and let her head droop against his shoulder and forget the party in order to lose herself completely in him.

She had to use the last bit of common sense she possessed to tear her gaze from his face and turn her head away. She realized gratefully that the waiter had returned to their table with their entrées.

Zack had seen, too. "Mighty inconvenient timing," he murmured as he guided her to the edge of the floor.

Brandi pretended not to hear, but her pulse was thumping madly. What had he been thinking just then? she wondered. And if they hadn't been in the middle of a crowded room, what might he have done?

As they sat down once more, Whitney studied them with an impartial, level gaze. It wasn't an unfriendly look, just an appraising one. Still, it made Brandi a bit nervous, and she tried to laugh as she said, "You usually look at things that way when you're considering damage control."

Whitney didn't answer. Instead she said, "I hear you had some excitement at the store the other night."

"You mean our robber?" Brandi tried a bit of her prime rib; it was so tender that the weight of the knife was almost enough to cut it. "I suppose next we'll have to start combat training for all employees."

"It's got to be a fluke," Whitney said.

"Would you want to take a chance?"

Zack said, "How's the employee doing?"

"Incredibly well, from what I can see." Brandi put her fork down. "I went to visit her this afternoon, and she insisted she'll be back to work tomorrow."

"So soon?"

"Don't look at me that way, Zack. I suggested she take a few extra days off, but she thinks the longer she stays away the more difficult it will be to come back, and it's hard to argue with that logic."

"Especially when you're short of help," Zack murmured.

"Exactly." It was the perfect opening to mention his habit of sending prospective employees up to personnel. "And as long as we're on the subject of employees, Zack..."

"Yes?"

Brandi thought better of it. That kind of discussion was far better held in private, and it seemed she'd lost any desire to delve into business tonight. "Never mind. We can talk about it later."

Zack smiled, and the talk moved on to other things. As soon as they'd finished dinner, he drew her back onto the dance floor. The band was playing a series of slow, soft, dreamy numbers, and Brandi had no idea what time it was when Zack shifted his hold on her in order to check his wristwatch.

"You don't have to do your last shift," she murmured.

Zack's voice was soft and lazy. "You *are* having a good time, aren't you? The store's been closed for hours. It's almost midnight."

"Really?" She was vaguely surprised that it didn't bother her much. "Are you afraid I'll turn into a pumpkin when the clock strikes twelve?"

"Do you usually?" He didn't wait for an answer. "The kids were planning to drive their baby-sitter nuts by trying to stay awake all night, and I told them I'd peek in at the stroke of midnight to find out how the slumber party's going. Want to come?"

She didn't even hesitate. "All right."

The room he'd come from much earlier that evening was quiet and shadowed now, the only light falling from a night-light on a desk in the corner. It was obviously a boy's room; he was curled up in the top bunk, under a coverlet decorated with cowboys. In the bottom bunk, surrounded by a couple of dozen dolls and stuffed toys, was the little girl Brandi had seen earlier. Her rosy cheeks were flushed, and her cheek was pillowed on the fat tummy of a furry panda bear. She'd kicked off her frilly quilt.

Zack tucked it back around her. "Baby-sitter one, kids zero," he murmured. "I didn't think they'd make it to midnight."

Brandi studied the softness in his face. "You're very attached to them, aren't you?"

"They're very special kids." He gave a last pat to the cowboy quilt and drew Brandi back into the hallway. In the quiet little nook at the top of the stairs he stopped and turned her to face him.

Almost automatically, Brandi put her hands on his chest—to keep a little distance between them, she thought. Or, perhaps, so she could feel his warmth and the strong beat of his heart through her palms.

Even in the dim light, the diamond cluster on her left hand sparkled. Zack caught her hand and turned it to watch the stones at play. Then he said quietly, "Allow me," and slid the ring from her finger. Brandi started to protest, but she hadn't finished forming the words when he slid it into place on her right hand instead. "That's much better," he murmured, and kissed the bare spot at the base of her engagement finger.

Brandi had never realized that was such a sensual spot. She gasped a little, and Zack let go of her hands and drew her into his arms.

In the space of an instant, Brandi considered all the reasons she shouldn't let him do this. Then she dismissed them. She relaxed into his embrace and raised her hands to cup his face and draw him down to her.

This was very different from the other times he'd kissed her. This time he seemed almost hungry, as if only she could satisfy the needs he felt, and the sensation rocked Brandi to her bones.

She didn't know how long he kissed her, only that it seemed forever and still wasn't long enough. When Zack raised his head, his voice was almost hoarse. "I need to talk to you. But this isn't the time or the place."

She couldn't speak; her throat had closed up. She shook her head, meaning to agree that this was hardly the best choice for a heart-to-heart discussion, but before she could do more, they heard footsteps coming up the stairs, and they moved apart just in time.

"There you are, Zack," said a jovial voice. Brandi didn't recognize the man; he must be one of the Claytons' friends, not a Tyler-Royale executive. "How are you enjoying the toy business? I wanted to ask you—"

Zack made an impatient gesture, as if to cut him short. Brandi knew exactly what he was feeling; she would have little patience right now with another discussion of bookkeeping systems. What she needed was a few minutes by herself to clear her head. "Excuse me," she murmured.

"I'll wait for you downstairs," Zack said, and Brandi slipped away for a moment to the cloakroom.

Whitney was seated at the dressing table, tipping her lashes with mascara. She looked at Brandi in the mirror, and her eyes narrowed slightly.

As if, Brandi thought guiltily, she can see the kisses still burning on my lips.

Whitney replenished her mascara wand and leaned closer to the mirror. "I should probably bite my tongue off rather than say this," she murmured, "but watch out for Zack."

Brandi didn't look at her; she dug through her bag in search of a lipstick. "Why? Don't you like him?"

"Of course I like him. Everyone likes him; he's perfectly charming, just as most love-'em-and-leave-'em guys are. But you never know what's he's up to. This whole Santa episode makes no sense whatever."

Brandi carefully outlined her lips. As casually as she could, as if it didn't matter, she said, "I thought maybe he was really working for Ross as the new trouble-shooter or something."

Whitney gave a genteel little snort. "I doubt you'd ever catch Zack doing anything that responsible." She snapped the catch of her handbag. "Watch out, Brandi." She left the room without waiting for an answer.

For a couple of minutes, Brandi was alone in the cloakroom, but then it began to fill once more. The laughter and heavy mix of perfumes made her head start to ache, and she went back out to the hallway.

Zack had already gone down to the party; the shadowed little nook at the top of the stairs was empty. Brandi paused for a second at the top of the steps, trying to regain her mental balance, when she heard a voice from the room across the hall from the cloakroom.

It was Whitney's voice, low and urgent, with a hard edge that made the hairs at the nape of Brandi's neck rise.

"What's going on, Ross?" Whitney said. "Zack wouldn't tell me the reasons, but I've mentored Brandi for years, and I have a right to know. Why have you planted Zack in that store?"

CHAPTER EIGHT

BRANDI'S hand closed on the newel post with a grip so tight it should have hurt, but she was too stunned to notice.

Just two nights ago she'd asked Zack if he'd been sent to investigate her store, and he'd denied it. He'd said straight out that the problems he was dealing with had nothing to do with the store, or with her. His troubles were his own, he'd said; the store was performing beautifully....

At least, that was what he'd seemed to say. And then he'd kissed her so intensely and thoroughly that Brandi had stopped thinking about her suspicions. She wondered now if that was why he'd kissed her—because it was the simplest way to distract her from an inconvenient line of thought. It had been a very effective move, if so.

But Zack had been lying. Or perhaps he had told the literal truth, but phrased his words so carefully that she'd missed the underlying reality. It didn't make any difference, really, which it was—the intent had been to deceive.

Or was it possible instead that Whitney was simply wrong?

Brandi seized on that explanation with relief. It was easier to dismiss Whitney's intuition and business experience than to believe Zack had lied to her. Whitney's judgment was at fault, that was the problem. For some reason Brandi didn't understand, Whitney had taken a dislike to Zack, and she was willing to believe the worst of him.

Now it all made sense.

Brandi had actually taken the first step on her way downstairs when Ross said quietly, "I have my reasons, Whitney. And I'm not able to discuss them with you at this point."

The words hit Brandi with the force of a pile driver. Then Whitney's suspicions, and her own, were the truth.

Zack had lied.

Before she could recover her balance, Brandi heard the creak of a hinge as the bedroom door started to open. Ross and Whitney were coming out.

Brandi couldn't risk meeting them just now. She was in no shape to confront her boss and ask for an explanation—not on a matter of this much importance. And she was not up to seeing concern and perhaps pity in her friend's eyes, either.

But she couldn't just run downstairs. She couldn't brave meeting Zack at this moment; she didn't have enough self-control for that. She would need a chance to sort out her thoughts before she did anything at all.

Without making a conscious decision, Brandi fled back to the cloakroom and extracted her coat from the pile on the bed. She waited a couple of minutes, giving Ross and Whitney a chance to return to the party, and then tried to make herself invisible as she slipped down the stairs. If she could just get outside before anyone noticed...

But luck wasn't with her. She was almost at the front door when Ross called, "Brandi! You're leaving already?"

She turned, keeping her head down and drawing her shoulders up till the high collar of her coat hid a good part of her face. "It's been a lovely party," she said, "but I'm sure you'll forgive me for ducking out. I've got another long day tomorrow." Her voice was huskier than she'd have liked, but she hoped he wouldn't notice. He didn't argue, and she nodded a goodbye and went outside.

The temperature seemed to have dropped like a rock during the hours she'd been inside—or perhaps it was just that shock and fear had made her more sensitive to the cold. As Brandi stood on the curb and waited for the valet to bring her car, she tried not to look over her shoulder. With any luck at all, Zack would still be waiting for her in the party rooms, unaware that she was running away.

Which was, she freely admitted, exactly what she was doing.

I need to talk to you, he'd said. Brandi wondered what he'd been planning to tell her. Would he confess? And if so, what sort of explanation would he have for why he had lied to her before?

Maybe tomorrow she could listen to him. Right now, she'd probably start screaming.

She could see her breath, but by the time the valet returned with her car, Brandi had stopped feeling the cold. No amount of chill in the air could match the frigid brittleness deep inside her.

Even the long drive across the city with the car's heater running full blast didn't warm her up. Once inside her apartment, she lit the gas fire with shaking fingers, and huddled in front of it.

Just a couple of hours ago she had been happier than she had been in years, so happy that all sense of time had vanished in the enjoyment of Zack's company, of the warm security of his arms around her, of the delicious sense that the world was a saner place when she was with him.

But he had lied to her, and now all the freedom, the enjoyment, the hope that she had thought he represented were gone.

Only once before in her life had she felt this confused, this upset, this frozen. Once before she had given her trust, and she had been betrayed.

But that time, she had believed that she had known the man she trusted. As it turned out, she'd been wrong, and the disillusionment she'd suffered had kept her from making the same mistake for years afterward. In fact, she'd thought the memory of her pain would keep her from repeating that particular error forever.

But it hadn't. In fact, this mistake was worse, if anything. She had never allowed herself to believe that she knew Zack at all—but still she had allowed herself to trust in him, to believe that he was different, special. The kind of man she could truly care about.

Brandi sat beside the fire, listening to the soft hiss and crackle of the flame, smelling the sharp pine fragrance of the garland Zack had so carefully fitted over the mantel two nights ago, and staring at the diamond-cluster ring that he had moved from her left hand to her right. It had been such a romantic gesture—such a touching, world-shaking signal that he was serious about her.

Oh, he was serious all right, she reflected. Serious about deceiving her.

She tugged the ring loose and put it back on the hand where it belonged. The hand where it would stay.

Brandi was in the store early the next day, though she had to admit that her almost-sleepless night had left her with less than her usual concentration.

She normally enjoyed Sunday mornings. The quiet hour before the employees started to come in was a perfect opportunity to walk through every department, undistracted by customer problems or employee concerns. On her normal walk-throughs, she was watching her people as much as the store itself. On Sundays she could concentrate on the merchandise, keeping a sharp eye out for displays that looked tired, mannequins that sagged, stacks that had been pushed out of line. It was tiny details like these that made Tyler-Royale stand out among other department stores, and Brandi was determined her store was going to be the cream of the crop.

But today it took effort to focus on the job. The store was too quiet, and her mind kept slipping back to the party the night before. Surprisingly, though, it wasn't only the abrupt end of the evening that seemed imprinted on her mind, but the earlier fun. Even the night before, with the pain still fresh and raw, whenever she had managed to close her eyes it hadn't been the shock at the top of the stairs she remembered, but the hypnotic rhythm of dancing with Zack....

And that kind of thinking, she told herself, was going to get her precisely nowhere.

She pulled her mind back to the task at hand. They were halfway through the Christmas season, and the biggest shopping days of the year were still to come. Did the store have enough stock in the areas that were selling best? Was there an excess of certain merchandise? If so, perhaps it should be marked down to speed its sale, or perhaps offered to other stores in the chain where the demand might be heavier.

The computer in her office would give her the numbers, of course, but Brandi had long ago learned to put more faith in her instinct than in statistics.

She paid particular attention to Toyland, since it was the busiest single department at this time of year. The stock was starting to drop, she noted, but so far there seemed no shortages anywhere. Extra supplies of toys and games were no longer stacked clear to the ceiling, but the regular shelves were still full and inviting.

She wondered which displays Zack was responsible for rearranging. He'd said something about games, hadn't he? There was a pile of board games laid out in an eye-catching pattern at the end of an aisle.

Not that it mattered, she told herself, and went on to electronics and housewares before she could dwell on the subject of Zack.

Before Brandi was quite finished with her tour, employees were coming in. The lights came up, the Christmas carols began to play, and soon the great doors opened and the first wave of customers poured in. Sundays during the Christmas season were always busy, but this was a particularly hectic day. Shopping urges that had been pent up by the week's snowstorm seemed to have been released in a frenzy.

Every department seemed to be overrun, and Brandi found herself pitching in on the floor, greeting customers in the atrium entrance, directing them to the merchandise they wanted, even ringing up sales for a while in the ladies' active-wear department, when Casey Amos and her new trainee—the woman Zack had discovered in the parking lot the night of the snowstorm—got behind.

Theresa Howard was apologetic. "I'm sorry I'm so slow, Ms. Ogilvie," she said. "Sometimes I think I'm all thumbs and I'll never learn this job."

Brandi smiled. "Casey and I have trained a lot of people," she reassured the woman. "You're doing just fine."

Finally the pressure let up. She showed Theresa Howard how to greet three customers at a time and still make each of them feel valuable, and then retreated to the executive floor, where the paperwork she'd intended to do before the store opened still waited.

But as she passed the customer service department, just down the hall from her office, Brandi saw that the two representatives were being run off their feet settling problems and wrapping packages. There was not only a line waiting for help, but a woman who wanted to apply for Wishing Tree assistance. Brandi took her off to a corner and went to work.

Where was Zack when she needed him? she thought irritably. There wasn't time to check the schedule to see if he was due to come in today—but she rather thought he was. She seemed to remember that the kooky schedule she'd arranged hadn't given him a single day off. Though, since she *had* told him last night that the schedule was more flexible than it implied, perhaps he'd decided to go back to setting his own hours.

Or maybe he didn't intend to come in to work at all. Maybe Whitney's question to Ross had tipped a balance somehow, and now that the secret was at least partially out, there was no further point in having Zack play his role.

Brandi wondered for the thousandth time what had happened last night after she'd left the party, and how long Zack had waited for her.

The client said hesitantly, "Excuse me?" and Brandi pulled herself away from the fascination of imagining the look on Zack's face when he realized she wasn't coming back.

"I really appreciate this, you know," the client said. "It's—well, it's the only way we'd have a Christmas, through the generosity of other people." Her voice was thick with emotion.

Brandi smiled sympathetically, but she didn't answer; she knew how close the woman was to tears. Instead she said gently, "What about you? Now that we've got the kids' lists made, what would you like?"

The woman shook her head. "Oh—nothing. The best gift for me will be if people care a little about my kids."

Brandi looked down at the form she had just finished filling out, and her eyes began to prickle uncontrollably. It was such a simple list—warm jeans and boots for a couple of little boys, and a snowsuit and a baby doll for a three-year old. "You'll get everything on your list," she said firmly.

A sudden tingle in the back of her neck warned her that Zack was somewhere around. She sneaked a look through her lashes and spotted him near the door of the employees' lounge. He was leaning against the wall and watching her.

Brandi found herself feeling hot and cold all over, and all at the same time. She tried not to look at him again, but it was impossible to keep her gaze from straying in his direction.

No Santa suit today. He was still dressed for the street, in a black leather jacket and jeans. His garb was the most casual she'd seen him wear, and it made him look tougher somehow—as if he no longer needed to project a sophisticated veneer.

The client thanked her, gave Brandi's hand a fierce squeeze, and left.

Brandi stacked the papers she'd filled out in a folder, fussing till she had them lined up just right. She didn't see Zack leave the lounge area and come toward her. She didn't have to; she could feel his closeness as easily as if she'd suddenly sprouted radar antennae.

He didn't take the chair across from her where the client had sat, but leaned against the table beside her instead, his hip almost brushing her arm. "Now who's making rash promises?" he said.

She tried to keep things casual. "It wasn't rash. I'll take care of it myself. You needn't even put those stars on the tree."

"Shopping and everything? You amaze me, Brandi."

She could feel his warmth, but there was no place to move. Her chair was already against the wall, and the dominating position he'd assumed not only blocked her from slipping past him but made her feel tiny and helpless.

Though Brandi wasn't about to admit that; no one was going to bully her simply by sitting on the edge of a table and looking down his nose. "The manager of the supermarket down at the other end of the mall offered to fix food baskets for our Wishing Tree people," she said. "You might want to go talk to him about it."

Zack nodded. He didn't speak, and he didn't move.

"I suppose you'd like to look over the application?" Brandi held out the folder. "I hope I did it to your standards."

Zack didn't reach for the paperwork. He folded his arms across his chest instead and looked down at her. She followed his gaze; he was looking at the diamond cluster on her left hand, and there was a shuttered wariness in his eyes that she'd never seen before.

She put the folder down. "Don't look at me like that, please. You know, I wouldn't have objected if you'd wanted to take over that job—it is your department after all."

"You were obviously almost finished." His voice had a rough edge. "Besides, I didn't want to take the chance that you'd scream and run if I approached you too suddenly."

"What?" Brandi was honestly at a loss.

"You didn't seem to want to talk to me last night," he reminded her.

"Well, I certainly wouldn't scream and run here."

"Oh, that's right." There was an edge of irony in his tone. "We're in the store now, and all the rules are different."

She watched him warily. He sounded angry—no, it was more than that. There was a tinge of bitterness in his voice, and that made Brandi furious. Did he honestly expect that he could lie to her and get away with it forever?

She was aware that the crush at the customer service counter had abated, leaving the clerks free to observe. She should probably take him back to her office and close the door and have it out.

Before she could suggest it, though, Zack said softly, "Why did you run away last night?"

She couldn't deny it, for it was true, she had run. But she wasn't going to let him put her on the defensive. "I don't owe you any explanations, Zack."

"What the hell does that mean? Of course you owe me an explanation! How do you think I felt when I discovered you'd slipped out without even telling me?"

"Guilty, maybe?" Brandi guessed.

There was a flicker in his eyes, as if the jab had struck deep into his soul. His voice grew softer, but it was no less resolute. "I told you I needed to talk to you, and you promptly vanished. Were you afraid to hear what I had to say, so you ran?"

"Maybe I just wasn't ready to listen to another round of lies just then."

"Lies?" The softness had vanished. "Dammit, Brandi—"

"Oh, come off it, Zack! The innocent act might still be convincing if I hadn't heard Ross telling Whitney last night that he planted you in my store."

"He said *what*?" Zack sounded astonished.

"She asked him why he'd put you in this store," Brandi said impatiently, "and he said he wasn't at liberty to tell her. Now correct me if I'm wrong, Zack, but a few days ago I asked you the same question, and you denied it—right?"

He shook his head a little, more in confusion than denial. "You asked me if I was Ross's troubleshooter, and I said no, I'm not. Which is the absolute truth."

"Oh, I beg your pardon! Perhaps I got the details a little askew, but—"

"I'm not here because of Ross, Brandi."

"Oh, really?" Her voice dripped sarcasm. "I suppose I imagined him telling me to hire you?"

"I mean, he suggested this particular store. But playing Santa was my idea."

"Well, maybe you should tell me what this is all about!" She didn't realize how shrill she sounded until she noticed both of the customer service representatives watching her intently, mouths ajar.

"I tried last night," Zack said. "You wouldn't listen."

Maybe he had intended to tell her, she thought wearily. She'd have to give him the benefit of the doubt on that question. "Well, I'm all ears now."

Zack glanced over his shoulder at the customer service representatives. "You and a lot of other people," he said dryly. "Perhaps we could go into your office?"

They were in Dora's alcove when the manager of Toyland came bursting out of the elevator. "Ms. Ogilvie!" he called. "There you are! I've been trying to find you."

Brandi paused. "What is it?"

"Not now," Zack said through gritted teeth. "Can't you, just once, let the store go to hell?"

She glared at him. "When I've got an undercover agent standing right here? Of course not!"

"And Zack," the department manager said with relief. "Man, am I glad to see you." He seized Zack's arm with both hands.

"If you're short a clerk, I'm sorry," Zack began. "But—"

The manager shook his head. "It's a whole lot worse than that. This afternoon's Santa came in to work all right, but he's in the dressing room now—as sick as anyone I've ever seen."

"The flu?" Brandi asked.

"Sure looks like it. He's far too sick to do his job—he'd expose every kid in the store to this bug. But there's a line from here to the moon waiting to talk to Santa. Zack, you'll help me out, won't you? I've got to have a Santa!"

Zack didn't answer.

Brandi looked up at him. His gaze was dark and steady and watchful, as if he was asking a silent question.

But there could be only one answer; the needs of the store came first. "I'll have to ask you to pitch in," she said levelly. "We'll talk later, Zack."

"You can bet on that." There was a steel thread underlying his voice.

Brandi put her chin up. "Believe me, I'm as eager as you are to get this sorted out. But in the meantime, look on the positive side. You'll have all afternoon to get your story straight!"

Brandi made it a point to be highly visible for the rest of the business day. Zack was not going to be able to accuse her of hiding away in her office. Besides, though she wouldn't have admitted it to him, she couldn't have settled down to her regular work if her life had depended on it.

Her mind was going a million miles a minute, trying to anticipate his explanation—but she couldn't think of any that made sense.

If he *wasn't* in the store because of Ross...but Ross had said quite plainly...

Give it up, Brandi, she told herself finally. She'd simply have to wait till she heard his side of it and make her judgment then.

She got caught up in a crowd on the escalator and her white carnation was smashed. She was in the employees' lounge, digging through the refrigerator for a replacement, when a couple of clerks came in to put their names into the jar for the Christmas gift exchange. "You're going to be in it this year, aren't you, Ms. Ogilvie?" one of them asked. "It's just good fun."

Brandi shook her head, but after the clerks were gone she pinned her flower in place and thought of what the Wishing Tree client had said—about how the best gift would be knowing that people cared.

Maybe she should take part, she thought. It was such a simple little thing. And it was Christmas after all— the time for caring.

Before she had a chance to argue herself out of it, she'd written her name on one of the little cards Casey Amos had left beside the jar and dropped it in.

She walked through Toyland several times during the afternoon, watching the line inching past Santa's Workshop, and happened to be there for the big stir of the day, when a couple brought in their infant quadruplets, dressed in identical red velvet suits, for their first visit with Santa.

"Makes quite a picture, doesn't it?" a bystander asked Brandi, chuckling at the sight. "Santa's got his hands full, holding all four of 'em at once."

She nodded and leaned against the fence to watch. The babies were three months old, their mother told her, and for a moment Brandi lost herself in sheer enjoyment not only of their antics but the way Zack handled them. The babies wriggled, made faces, and yanked at his beard; Zack watched them with a tenderness in his face that tugged at Brandi's heart.

Then he looked up and caught her eye, and the tenderness faded, to be replaced with something that looked more like a challenge—and Brandi stepped away from the fence and almost tripped over her own feet in her eagerness to be away.

Last night he had held her and kissed her, and he had seemed to say that he had serious feelings about her. For why would a man move a ring from her left hand, unless he intended to make room for a more important one?

But today... today he had looked at her almost with scorn.

Closing time approached, and the crowds began to thin. Brandi waited beside the perfume counter nearest the main entrance till a customer turned away with a bag full of fragrances.

The clerk was back at work as she had promised. Brandi thought she looked a little shaky, as if she wasn't quite over her shock. That would be no surprise, she thought, and wondered if she should have refused permission to let the woman come back just yet.

But the clerk greeted her with a wide smile. "It's good to be back," she said. "I wondered if I'd have the jitters all day, but it hasn't been bad at all. Of course, it's been busy, and that helps."

The clerk turned away to help a customer, a long-haired young woman wearing faded jeans and a canvas vest, its pockets stuffed with odds and ends. "I'd like an ounce of Sensually Meghan," she said, and pulled a credit card out of her back pocket.

Brandi's eyebrows went up just a fraction of an inch. The woman didn't look like the Sensually Meghan type— that particular scent cost three hundred dollars an ounce these days. It was just another example demonstrating that customers couldn't be judged by appearance. She made a mental note to mention the incident at the next full staff meeting as encouragement to her employees not to jump to conclusions based on a customer's clothes.

The clerk was processing the charge when the customer asked, "How long does it usually take after closing for all the people to clear out of the mall?"

Brandi's sixth sense started to quiver. "On Sundays, not long," she said. "Why?"

The woman smiled at her. "It is an odd question, isn't it? We work for an advertising agency." She gestured toward the main entrance, where two men with video cameras waited. "We'll be shooting footage for ads for the mall."

Brandi relaxed. Really, she thought, since the robbery attempt, I'm starting to get paranoid.

"We don't want our equipment to get in the way," the young woman went on, "but frankly, we're not wild about working Sunday nights, either, so if we time it just perfectly we can shoot and get out and not annoy anyone."

"I think I'd get started setting up," Brandi advised. "If you're off to the side of the main doors, no one will trample you."

"Hey, thanks." The customer stuck her expensive perfume carelessly into a pocket and headed for the entrance.

"You just never know, do you?" the clerk said.

The public address system crackled to life and announced that the store was now closed, and the clerk began to clear the cash register. Brandi dug out her keys and went to shut the big metal gates that barricaded the Tyler-Royale store from the rest of the mall.

She stopped the gate just short of full closure to allow procrastinating shoppers an exit, and watched the camera crew setting up their tripods and lights just outside the store.

But her mind wasn't on them, but on the coming confrontation with Zack.

Thinking of him seemed to have the power to conjure him up, for just a couple of minutes after the closing announcement she saw him coming down the now-stationary escalator. He was still wearing his Santa suit.

"I'd have waited for you to change," she said as he came up to her.

"Then I will. I saw you hovering down here as if you were ready to run, and I thought perhaps—"

He broke off as a scream sliced through the air.

Brandi looked around frantically. The only thing she was certain of was that the sound hadn't originated anywhere inside Tyler-Royale. Sound echoed oddly in the huge open mall, however, and the scream could have come from a hundred places.

Just outside the gate, a member of the camera crew said, "What the—"

Another scream sounded, and a man erupted from the cookie and snack shop next door to Tyler-Royale and started down the length of the mall at a dead run. Under his arm was what looked like a brown paper bag.

The perfume clerk gasped, "That's the guy who tried to rob me!"

Zack shot one look at the clerk, pushed Brandi out of his way, and took off after the robber.

Propelled by the push, Brandi collided with the metal gate and grabbed the rods to keep herself upright. She was shrieking something; she thought it was his name.

Time seemed to stretch out in slow motion as she clung to the gate and watched the chase. Ever so slowly, stride by stride, Zack gained on the man with the bag, till with one final lunge he slammed a shoulder into the robber's back, and the two of them went down together onto the hard tile floor.

As they rolled, Brandi saw the flash of metal in the robber's hand. Was he holding a knife? A gun?

In her terror for Zack, she screamed again. It was a useless warning for him, but a blinding revelation for her.

As the two man grappled for the weapon, Brandi knew, with the terrible clarity that sometimes comes with shock, that it didn't matter to her what Zack had done, or who he was, or why he was in her store. Or even whether he had lied to her after all.

That was all unimportant, less than nothing beside the fact that somehow, while she wasn't even looking— much less protecting herself—Zack Forrest had crept into her heart.

Last night she had been hurt by the discovery that she had let herself trust him despite her lack of knowledge of what he really was. Now that discovery paled beside the blinding realization that this was not only a man she could care about if the circumstances worked out just right, but the one and only man she loved.

CHAPTER NINE

THE struggle in the mall could only have lasted for a minute or two, but to Brandi it seemed to go on for years. Where were the mall security guards? she wanted to scream. What good did it do to have people on the staff if they weren't there when they were needed?

Finally, the guards converged on the pair in the hall. Two of them sat on the robber; another helped Zack stand up. Logic told Brandi he wasn't hurt after all, for the first thing he did was to dust off his red velvet suit.

Nevertheless, she was still shaking minutes later when the camera crew came triumphantly down the corridor. She hadn't even noticed they were gone, and she paid little attention to the video cassette the young woman in the canvas vest was waving over her head.

"What a piece of action!" she was saying. "We'll be on the news on every station in greater Chicago. Santa Claus busts a robber, and we've got it on tape!" She grinned at Brandi. "What can you tell me about your Santa—besides that he's in great shape under the velvet suit?"

Brandi noticed with almost clinical detachment that each of her fingertips was quivering to a different rhythm. "Not much," she said. "His name's Zack Forrest, and he's a temporary employee, just for the season. That's all I really can—"

"Zack Forrest?"

Something about the woman's tone made Brandi's eyes narrow in suspicion. "That's what I said, yes."

"You mean the toycoon?"

"What did you call him?"

"*Toycoon*. It's the nickname Wall Street gave him last spring when he bought Intellitoys. You know, the educational-toy maker."

The little oxygen still in Brandi's lungs rushed out with a whoosh. *How's the toy business*? one of their fellow guests had asked Zack last night. Brandi had thought the guest meant the Santa job.... Zack owned a toy company?

"We were shooting an ad for one of their new products last week," the young woman went on, "and I did my research. I wonder what he's up to? Why's he playing Santa anyway?"

From the corner of her eye, Brandi glimpsed a red suit, and she turned around to get a better look.

Zack's hair was ruffled, and his fake beard hung askew. He'd lost his velvet cap in the fracas, and he sounded as if he was still a little breathless. "I'm just doing my volunteer stint for the children," he said, and smiled at the woman who held the videotape.

Brandi was torn between the desire to fling her arms around him and kiss the dimple in his cheek in gratitude that he was safe, or slap him across the face as hard as she could for taking a foolish risk.

"Perhaps I'm being immodest to ask," Zack went on, "but am I the star of that videotape you're waving around?"

The young woman grinned. "Yeah. You can watch yourself on TV tonight—I bet every station in the city will want this. Maybe even the networks."

"Ah," Zack said knowingly. "Doing a little moon-lighting, are you?"

"Anything wrong with that?" A defensive note crept into the woman's voice. "There's no clause in my contract with the advertising agency that forbids me to make a little money on the side.''

"Of course there's nothing wrong with a little enlightened capitalism," Zack soothed. "Though, as long as the tape's for sale..." He reached for his wallet. "How much do you think they'll pay? And how many stations are there?"

The woman told him, and then looked at him incredulously while Zack counted a series of bills into her hand.

"There," he said. "And a little extra for good measure. You've turned a profit, and this way you don't even have to mess around making copies for all the stations." The videotape vanished into a capacious pocket of the red velvet suit, and Zack looked around with a smile. "I think you might want to reschedule your regular business, though. It looks as if the mall will be tied up for a while tonight."

In the meantime, Brandi saw, the police had arrived in force. She watched while they cordoned off the snack shop and the videotape crew packed up their equipment and left.

Only then did she speak, still without looking at Zack. "What are you planning to do with the videotape?"

"Haven't decided. But it was obviously a once-in-a-lifetime opportunity, so I thought I'd better grab it while I could."

"You could always show it at parties. I'm sure it would be a hit."

"Now that's a thought," Zack said agreeably. "People who don't know that's the most incompetent robber in the Western hemisphere would think I looked like a hero."

Brandi nodded. Her voice was perfectly calm. "That was a sizable amount of money you just handed over for someone who implied a few days ago that he couldn't quite keep up with the payments on his car.''

Zack had the grace to look ashamed of himself.

Brandi didn't wait for an answer. She looked straight at him, and fury hardened her voice. "Dammit, Zack, why didn't you tell me who you are? Or what you do? Why the big secret?''

His tone was even and perfectly calm. "Because I didn't want to advertise the fact that Intellitoys is in big trouble.''

She shook her head more in confusion than disagreement. It seemed such an inadequate reason.

A burly policeman came up to them. "Uh...Santa. We'll need a statement from you, sir.''

For a moment Zack ignored him; he was watching Brandi. Finally he sighed and said, "I'll be back as soon as I can, Brandi.''

"I'll be in my office.''

It was more than an hour before he tapped perfunctorily on the door and came in. He'd taken the time to change clothes, she saw, and he was once more wearing the jeans and leather jacket he'd had on when they'd started this conversation earlier in the afternoon.

It felt to Brandi as if that had been a very long time ago. Back then, she'd known only that he had the power to hurt her. But she hadn't understood how deep that power ran, or how devastating the hurt could be. She hadn't yet realized that she loved him, and she hadn't begun to conceive of the deception he'd practiced.

Now she felt as if he'd torn her heart from her chest without bothering with anesthesia.

She'd been trying to concentrate on a supplier's catalog with little success. She put it down when Zack came in, but she didn't say a word.

Neither did Zack; he pulled a chair around and straddled it, his arms crossed on the back. Brandi wasn't surprised that he felt as if he needed a shield.

For a full minute it seemed as if they might sit that way forever. Silent as the confrontation was, however, the air between them seemed to sizzle.

When Zack finally spoke, it was almost as if he was picking up in the middle of a conversation. "Intellitoys' advance orders for the Christmas season were reasonable," he said quietly. "Not good, but acceptable. But as the holiday got closer, we started getting cancellations from stores because merchandise they already had on hand wasn't selling. And soon a fair performance was turning into a disaster. We could absorb a single season of low sales, even a Christmas season, but there was a larger problem—nobody seemed to know why the sales were down. And unless a company knows why it's not selling merchandise, next year is apt to be nothing but worse."

Brandi fidgeted with a paper clip. She couldn't argue with that logic as far as it went. She just didn't understand what it was supposed to have to do with her.

"It was apparent to anyone with eyes that the marketing firm we were using didn't have a clue," Zack went on. "They kept saying it was just a cyclical drop that would correct itself with time, but we haven't got that kind of time to play with. The company could be dead and buried by the time they'd admit they might be wrong."

Brandi knew the helpless feeling he must have suffered—knowing action was required, but not knowing which direction to move.

"So I fired them," Zack said. "It was an impulsive decision, I admit, but it left me no worse off than I was before."

Brandi didn't intend to rescue him, but she couldn't help but agree with that philosophy. "Bad information is worse than having none at all."

Zack smiled approvingly, as if she were a particularly bright student. "Very true. But firing the marketers didn't solve the problem, either—we still had to somehow find out what was going wrong. Why did kids suddenly not seem to want our products, and why had parents lost interest, as well?"

"So you decided to become a Santa?" Brandi shifted restlessly in her chair. "Pardon me for questioning your judgment, Zack, but there's more than one marketing firm in the world. Couldn't you just hire another one and use focus groups? Get a bunch of kids and parents into a room and ask them what they like? Putting on a red suit and a beard is just about the silliest—"

"Oh, is it really? Focus groups are no more honest than statistics, you know—it's not at all hard to skew the results, even with the best of intentions. I figured I'd ask the real authorities—the kids themselves, and the parents. And how better to get their honest feelings than to sit in Santa's chair?"

"It's not what you'd call a scientific sample."

"Scientific samples take time, which I haven't got. Right now, I don't need analysis, I need a gut reaction of what's wrong. Which, I might add, I started getting the first day I was out there."

"With a notebook," Brandi reflected.

"You'd better believe I was taking notes. I didn't want to forget a single comment because that's a good way to be led astray, too. It's easy to remember only what you want to."

"And you think you've got the answers?"

"No—but I know which direction we need to go." There was confidence in his voice.

Brandi sighed. There wasn't much point in arguing with him; Zack was convinced he'd taken the right course. In any case, it didn't matter, because his reasons for starting this masquerade weren't really important. "So why didn't you tell me what you were up to?" she asked softly.

He shook his head as if in disbelief of her innocence. "The stock-market wizards would have been on me like the sharks they are. With the first drop of blood, those guys go into a feeding frenzy. That in turn would have very nasty effects on my stockholders' confidence level."

"No doubt, but—"

"What would you think if the president of the biggest manufacturer of light bulbs in this country showed up at the corner drugstore demonstrating them, and asking people why they suddenly seemed to prefer other brands to his?"

Brandi shook her head. "No. You're telling me why you didn't want it known, and I understand all the reasons. But that's not what I asked, Zack. Why didn't you tell *me*?"

He seemed to be staring at his feet. "It was important that I be just an ordinary Santa," he said. "A working stiff with no stake in the answers I got. People are amazingly adaptable at telling a survey taker what they think he wants to hear. If I stood out in any way, it would affect what I was trying to accomplish."

As if this unlikely Santa hadn't stood out from the beginning, Brandi thought wryly. "And just what did you think I was apt to do? Call a press conference and announce your little project?"

"I didn't know you, Brandi," he said softly. "How could I possible have had the answer to that question?"

And what about later, she wanted to ask. What about after he'd had a chance to get to know her?

But too many of the possible answers to that question scared her. She didn't think she could stand to sit there, loving him as she did, and listen as he told her that he still didn't trust her to keep his secrets—at least, not enough to volunteer them without being forced.

And so she didn't ask.

"It was safer if you didn't know," Zack went on. "No one could get information out of you if you didn't know it in the first place."

The gentle note in his voice made her want to hit him; the desire was even stronger than it had been a couple of hours ago, right after that crazy stunt he'd pulled.

"Ross thought it was better if nobody knew. That way there couldn't be a slipup."

Brandi swallowed hard. "So Ross didn't trust me, either?"

"It's not that, Brandi. Honestly, it's not. But Ross is a major stockholder in Intellitoys, and if it got out that he was worried about the company..."

There was no need to finish that sentence. Once Wall Street got hold of that information, there would be nothing left of Intellitoys but splinters.

"Or, for that matter," Zack went on, "if the other toy companies that Tyler-Royale deals with discovered that Ross was favoring my business over theirs by using his stores as a laboratory, they'd be unhappy."

That was an understatement. Brandi knew from long experience what suppliers could be like if they thought someone else was getting an unfair break. She shivered.

"I see you understand the problem," Zack said. "Even Tyler-Royale's board of directors might well have had a collective fit. Maybe Ross was wrong to keep you out of the loop, Brandi—"

"*Maybe*? Didn't it occur to either of you that if I knew, it might keep me from saying something I shouldn't?"

"Yes. But you must admit, right or not, Ross had good reason for asking me to stay under wraps."

Brandi thought it over, and finally nodded. She still thought Ross and Zack had been wrong, but she didn't have to agree in order to understand.

But somehow, she thought, she was never going to feel quite the same about Ross Clayton again. And as for Zack ... well, she'd have to think about that one for a good long time.

"So that's why Ross wouldn't tell Whitney what was going on," she mused.

"If he thought you didn't need to know," Zack said reasonably, "why would he be willing to tell Whitney?"

She couldn't argue with the logic of that, either, but it made her furious that she couldn't find a flaw in his reasoning.

Zack's voice was soft. "I wanted to tell you, Brandi, when you asked me about the troubleshooter and whether the store was in trouble. But it wasn't altogether up to me. You understand, don't you, that it was Ross's secret as much as mine? I couldn't spill it without warning him."

And that, Brandi thought wearily, told her exactly where she ranked, didn't it? Well down toward the bottom of his list.

Suddenly the office felt stuffy, as if they'd used up all the oxygen, and she felt an almost overpowering need to get out of the store and into the fresh cold air.

"Goodness knows I understand putting business first," Brandi said crisply. "In fact, it's nice to know that you have enough sense to do that—at least when it's *your* business that's concerned." She knew she sounded a bit catty, and she didn't care. "I think we've covered everything, don't you?" She stood up and came around the corner of the desk. It was the most obvious dismissal she could imagine.

Zack put a hand out toward her.

She took a half step back, well out of his reach. "Or is there something else you'd like to tell me, Zack?"

For a moment, his eyes looked cloudy, as if he was staring into the distance at something she couldn't see. Then his dark gaze focused once more on her face. "No."

"Then I suppose the only thing left is to agree on an explanation of why you're suddenly not playing Santa anymore."

Zack didn't move. "Why?"

"To avoid any uncomfortable questions, of course. Would you rather I say you've had a job offer you couldn't turn down, or that illness in the family called you away? Either way, I could imply you've gone out of state. Or maybe that's not far enough. How about out of the country?"

"I'm not planning to quit now, Brandi."

"You certainly can't keep on."

"Why not? I'm not finished. I told you I've got direction now, but not answers. Ross agreed with me that you'd have to know, but there's no need to bring anyone else into it."

"Wouldn't you be better off finishing your research somewhere else?"

Zack looked up at her for a long moment. His eyes had narrowed, and they looked darker than she'd ever seen them before. "You really want me to leave, don't you? Why, Brandi? Is it because I'm some kind of threat to your peace of mind?"

"A threat? To me? That's a joke." To her own ears, Brandi's voice lacked conviction. "But if you insist, stay.

Goodness knows, I don't want to take chances with my career by making Ross mad at me.''

Zack didn't seem to hear her. "You haven't answered my question yet about why you didn't stick around and listen to me last night.''

She shrugged. "The delay doesn't seem to have made much difference. Or isn't this what you were planning to tell me?''

He hesitated, and then said quietly, "Not exactly.''

He no doubt meant he'd had an edited version in mind till he'd been caught out and had to tell the whole story. Well, that didn't surprise her. "If you'll excuse me, Zack, I still have work to do.'' She sat down behind her desk again and picked up the catalog she'd been holding when he came in. She couldn't even remember what she'd been looking at.

He stood and slid the chair into position across from her. "Then I'll see you tomorrow.''

Only if I don't see you first, Brandi thought.

If she'd had more energy, Brandi would have pulled the pine garland down from the mantel, shredded it needle by needle, and flung it like confetti over the rail of her apartment balcony to mulch the garden below.

If the fireplace had been real instead of merely a gas log, she'd have stuffed the garland in and set a match to it, and sent the whole thing up in one explosive puff of resin.

But perhaps it was just as well that she didn't; demolishing the garland might have been cathartic, but Brandi knew the memories it represented would not be so easily destroyed. As long as she lived, she would remember the night Zack had so carefully draped the greenery—and then kissed her, to cover up... not an outright lie, perhaps, but certainly a half truth.

Part of the trouble was that she truly understood the position he'd been in. He'd given his word in a matter of business, and an honorable man didn't go back on that. She understood that Zack had been caught in a situation where he couldn't—technically—do anything at all. He couldn't tell her the truth without first warning Ross, but he couldn't tell her anything else without lying, at least by implication.

The same thing had happened to her on occasion, and she'd handled it the same way. So how could she blame him for doing what he'd had to do?

But her heart still told her that if he had cared about her...

Stop tormenting yourself this way, she told herself. Loving wasn't always reciprocal—hadn't she learned even that much from Jason?

She'd cared desperately about him, that was sure. After it was over and the pain had receded, she'd realized that perhaps her desperation had been even stronger than her caring. She'd lost her mother not long before, and she'd needed someone to make her feel valuable, connected to the world. Jason had been quite happy to fulfil that role—as long as it was convenient, and as long as Brandi had required nothing more serious of him.

But Zack was different, and she'd known it at some level all along—even while she'd thought that the experience with Jason would keep her safe. Even when she'd thought Zack was just another careless, happy-go-lucky young man out for a good time with little thought for the future, somewhere deep inside her heart she'd recognized how different he was.

Jason would never have challenged her decisions, her orders, as Zack had; it would have been too much trouble. Jason had never fussed about the hours she worked, for it gave him time to tinker with his novel;

Zack had seemed worried about her. Jason had often told her how proud he was of her independence; he would never have cared for her as tenderly as Zack had—taking her home, walking her to her car, making sure she wasn't alone at the party.

Jason had been a cardboard figurine. Only after he was gone from her life did Brandi realize how little she had known him, and how much of the man she thought she'd loved had been constructed from her own imaginative longings.

But Zack...Zack was a living, breathing, three-dimensional man. Sometimes difficult, often opinionated, always challenging.

But always lovable. That would never change.

On Tuesday, her secretary came into Brandi's office with a computer printout and a worried expression. "You know how we open a charge account automatically for every new employee?" she began.

Brandi nodded impatiently. "What about it, Dora?"

"We've got a new hire who's charged almost up to the limit."

Brandi put out a hand for the printout. "One of Zack's finds from the Wishing Tree project, no doubt?"

"No. It's Zack himself."

What a way to hide out, Brandi thought. For a man who said he wanted no special treatment—nothing that would distinguish him from the ordinary employee—Zack was hardly fading into the wallpaper. Of course, Zack could create a storm in a teacup and probably never realize it. He was so supremely confident of himself that he thought everyone else was just as self-assured.

But she wasn't going to get caught up in thinking about his attributes today, she reminded herself.

She ran an eye down the list. Most of the charges were on the small side, but there were a lot of them. No wonder Dora's attention had been drawn to this; what was the man thinking of?

Brandi sighed. "I'll talk to him. In the meantime, I don't think you need to worry about it."

Dora looked doubtful, but she didn't argue. Brandi went back to work, but the printout on the corner of her desk seemed to be looking at her, and finally she couldn't stand it for another minute. She'd managed to avoid him since Sunday, but she would have to seek him out now.

It was the dinner hour, so he was apt to be down in Santa's Workshop, filling in during the break. She picked up the printout and took the escalator to the second floor.

The crowd was small tonight; in fact, just one man in a trench coat and a couple of small children were inside the fence that surrounded Santa's Workshop. The man was chatting with Zack while the kids climbed all over him.

She set the "Santa's Feeding His Reindeer" sign in place and closed the gate. Zack looked up as if her presence was magnetic, and Brandi felt her heartbeat flutter a little under his steady gaze.

The man in the trench coat turned, and only then did Brandi realize it was Ross Clayton. "Hi, Brandi. Is it time for Zack's dinner?"

"No. I just needed to talk to him a minute."

Ross grinned. "I'll get my angels out of the way, then. I'll give you a call this week, Brandi. There are a couple of things we need to talk about."

She nodded. No doubt Zack had told him how upset she was. Well, that was all right; she still had a few things to say to Ross about this whole affair, and the sooner the air was cleared, the better.

Zack slid the little girl off his knee and stood up. The child took two steps toward Brandi. "I remember you," she announced. "You were at the party."

Brandi nodded. "You have a very good memory, Kathleen."

The child nodded without self-consciousness. "Uncle Zack said maybe we could see you again and help put up your Christmas tree. Then he said he didn't think so after all. Why not?"

Brandi shot a glance at him. What had he been planning anyway?

Before Brandi could answer, Kathleen's brother, with the arrogance of a couple of extra years, announced, "Because it's too late, dummy. Everybody's got their Christmas trees up by now."

"Don't call your sister a dummy," Ross said.

"Even if she is?"

Ross gave Brandi a crooked grin. "See all the fun you're missing by not having kids?"

It was a teasing comment, of course, but Brandi watched them till they were out of sight. She felt lonely, as if she'd thrown away something she hadn't even looked at yet—and only now realized that it was too late to change her mind.

Uncle Zack said maybe we could see you again and help put up your Christmas tree . . .

Brandi closed her eyes and remembered her brief vision of a track set up under a decorated tree, with a couple of children watching blissfully as a train went round and round, and Zack—

Stop it, she told herself. Just stop it.

"I thought Ross didn't want them to see you in costume," she said.

"Oh, they overheard some talk about my new job, so he thought it would be better for them to see me in the role than use their imaginations."

"They seemed to take it well."

"Maybe it's the fact that I've been trying toys out on them for months, so it seems an appropriate job for me to have."

"I see." She stuck her hands in her pockets; her fingertips brushed the folded computer printout and reminded her of why she'd come downstairs. "I need to warn you that you've just about exhausted your credit limit. If you need an increase, I'm afraid you'll have to convince the credit manager that you have resources beyond what we're paying you." There was a faintly ironic note in her voice.

Zack ignored it. "That's all right. I didn't feel I should profit financially from this little experience, so I've been buying some extras for the Wishing Tree. I'll just turn over my paycheck to pay the bills, and we'll be square."

Brandi nodded. "All right." The public address system crackled to life, and Dora asked her to come to the office. Great timing, Brandi thought; she couldn't have planned it better if she'd tried. "I'll see you later, then."

She hadn't quite met his eyes the whole time she'd been standing there, and she didn't intend to. It would be not only too painful, but too revealing. But as she turned to leave, he said her name, and the note of longing in his voice sabotaged all her intentions.

"I've missed you," Zack said huskily.

Brandi couldn't deny the ring of truth in his voice. And she could see desire in his eyes. He wanted to kiss her, and every cell in her body knew it and was recalling precisely how it had felt to be in his arms, to be held and caressed and kissed till nothing mattered but him....

"I thought maybe we had something special," Zack said.

Brandi swallowed hard. "Not without some trust."

He nodded. "I was wrong not to tell you."

"You certainly were."

"I'm sorry."

Every nerve was tingling. Was he really saying what she thought he might be—what she hoped he was telling her—that these few days of separation had made him realize, as she had, that he cared? *I thought maybe we had something special*, he'd said. Was it possible there was a second chance after all?

The last remaining fragment of common sense reminded her that this wasn't exactly a private spot for a conversation, much less anything more. Zack certainly couldn't kiss her right outside Santa's Workshop, in full view of every kid and parent in Toyland. Could he?

She couldn't help it; the urge to sway toward him was an irresistible one.

At the gate, a child cried, "But there's Santa! He's not gone after all!" and sanity returned with a snap.

"Later," Zack said.

Brandi nodded and hurried away. He hadn't even touched her, but her skin was tingling as if electrical jolts were running through her. Later, she thought dreamily, when the store was closed and the kids were gone, they could explore what he'd meant. What they meant to each other.

In the alcove outside Brandi's office, Dora looked relieved to see her. "I was starting to fret that you hadn't heard the page," she said. "Mrs. Townsend's on the telephone for you. She said she'd hold as long as it took, but—"

Brandi had forgotten all about Dora's summons. Feeling guilty, she hurried into her office and grabbed the phone. "Whitney? I'm sorry I took so long."

"Don't fret about it. I'd have waited forever."

There was a tense, almost harsh edge to Whitney's voice that scared Brandi. "What's going on?"

"I found out what Zack's up to."

Brandi relaxed. She turned her chair around, propped her heels on the corner of her desk, and considered how much to tell Whitney. She wouldn't volunteer that Intellitoys was in trouble, of course—but how much did Whitney already know?

Thank heaven Zack had told her everything, she thought. If he hadn't, she might have said the wrong thing just now and destroyed his plans—and maybe even his business.

"A little extra market research," Brandi said airily. "Finding out what kids want for Christmas. I know all about it."

"Oh, that much was obvious." Whitney's voice dripped impatience. "Good heavens, before he bought the company he was asking all the kids he ran into for their opinion of Intellitoys, so of course a stint as Santa would be right up his alley. But there's more, Brandi."

She means the drop in sales, Brandi told herself. But she couldn't quite make herself believe it. There was a black hole of dread in the pit of her stomach.

"I asked Ross last weekend why he'd planted Zack in your store," Whitney said, "and he wouldn't tell me."

Brandi didn't mean to admit to anything at all, but before she could stop herself she said, "I know." Her voice was little more than a croak.

"What did you say? Anyway, he wouldn't tell me right then. He was keeping his mouth shut because he knew I'd do exactly what I'm doing right now—I'd call you up and warn you. But now that he's made up his mind..."

Brandi's palms were damp. "*Warn* me? About what?" She could hardly force the words past the lump in her throat. Then there was something wrong! What disaster was about to descend on her?

Surely, she thought, she ought to *know*. Simply admitting that she didn't have the vaguest idea what was going on was tantamount to confessing that she wasn't fit to manage a store!

"Ross is going to offer you the job as his troubleshooter."

For a moment, Brandi thought she couldn't possibly have heard correctly. That wasn't a disaster; that was a promotion beyond even her craziest dreams.

She said, "I never in my life considered that."

"Well, think it over before you jump," Whitney said dryly. "Don't let yourself be awestruck into taking it. It's not all that great a job, aside from the fact that it puts you straight on the fast track to the head office."

Brandi shook her head a little. "Is that what you're warning me about—that the job has its disadvantages?"

"Not entirely." Whitney sighed. "In fact, that's not it at all, and this isn't going to be easy. Ross knows you're a good manager, but the next step up is a big one, and he wasn't so sure you were ready for it. So he sent Zack out there to do a little undercover work to see whether you had the right qualities to move up to the next level. Watch out for Zack, Brandi. He's there to spy on you."

CHAPTER TEN

BRANDI'S brain felt frozen. *Is there anything else you'd like to tell me*, she'd asked him. And Zack had said no, there wasn't.

Of course not, Brandi thought. He wouldn't *like* to tell her that his main reason for being in her store was to spy on her. Accidentally, she'd phrased the question so he could answer it with total truthfulness and still not be honest. He must have loved that!

"I'm terribly sorry to do this to you," Whitney said. "It's a rough blow, but perhaps it's better that you know it now. I could tell just from seeing you with Zack that you'd gone head over heels where he's concerned—"

"Head over heels? Don't be silly." Brandi's voice was a little shrill.

"Listen, kid, don't try to fool me. I know you too well. I just wish I'd found this out earlier."

"That makes two of us," Brandi admitted wearily. There was an instant of sympathetic silence, and Brandi, fearful of what Whitney might say next, hastily changed the subject. "There's something I don't understand about all this. How could I possibly be Ross's troubleshooter? I could hardly go under cover because everybody in the chain knows me."

"They know your name, but your habit of avoiding corporate parties works to your advantage. Not all that many people would recognize you on sight. Besides, troubleshooters don't stay anonymous for long, Brandi. About fifteen minutes after the job's offered, the grapevine starts spreading the word. You think everyone in the whole chain didn't know me?''

''I always thought—''

''And don't overestimate the amount of secret work that's to be done. Most of the time it's pretty straightforward. It's not an easy job, though—it wears people out and burns them up, and it doesn't take long for travel to lose its glamor. I held that job for almost three years, and I think my record stands to this day. But if that's what you want...''

Brandi considered the warning in Whitney's voice. But there really was only one answer she could give when the question was asked; this promotion was what she had worked for and dreamed of. It was another important step up the ladder to ultimate success. She had earned it, and she deserved to enjoy it. It was impossible to consider turning down such a plum.

''It's what I've always wanted,'' Brandi said quietly.

''Then you have my very best wishes, my friend. But at least think it over before you jump.''

Brandi thanked her and put down the telephone. She should be feeling wildly elated, she told herself. All her hard work had finally landed her on the fast track to the top of the corporation. Someday she might even sit in the office that was Ross Clayton's now, as the head of the whole chain.

When the shock wore off, she told herself, she'd be happy about her promotion. But just now, her head was spinning with fury and disappointment and sadness.

By the time Brandi came out of her office, Dora had gone; the lights were still on in the alcove, but the computer was hooded and her desk was neat. Down on the second floor, the Santa with the half glasses had returned from his dinner and taken his place in the big green wing chair outside the Workshop. Beneath his white whiskers, his face still looked a little pale from his bout with the flu, and Brandi wondered if she should send him home despite the doctor's release that said he was fit to return to work.

He greeted her with a smile, however, and a hearty Santa chuckle. "If you're looking for your young man, Ms. Ogilvie, he's back in the dressing room."

Your young man. The words fed the flames of Brandi's irritation. Did everyone in the store think that she was helplessly in love with Zack Forrest? Even Zack? Had he, perhaps, fed that rumor on purpose? Maybe it was even part of his effort to predict how she'd handle the stress of the new job!

She might not be able to wipe him out of her heart as easily as she'd like, but she could certainly put a stop to this nonsense. She could make it clear to everyone that they were not, and were never likely to be, a couple.

Brandi stalked around behind Santa's Workshop to the dressing-room entrance and, without pausing to think, yanked the door open.

Zack was standing with his back to her, tucking in the tail of his long-sleeved shirt. He half turned and grinned at her. "Hi, there. Is it my imagination, or are you a little impatient to get out of the store tonight?"

"I need to talk to you."

His eyebrows rose a little at her tone. "Give me a minute to put my shoes on," he said. "I'd invite you in, but as you can see, there's hardly room for both of us."

He was right. Santa's Workshop was a masterpiece of illusion. The interior was much smaller than the structure looked from the outside, and a closet and dressing table took up the majority of the dressing room's space. The ceiling was scarcely high enough to clear Zack's head.

Next Christmas, Brandi thought, they really ought to make it larger. But of course, next Christmas it wouldn't be her concern.

"Something wrong?" Zack inquired.

He actually sounded as if he didn't have a suspicion, and Brandi's exasperation rose another notch. She leaned against the door frame and folded her arms across her chest. "You know, Zack," she said, trying to keep her voice light, "I can't make up my mind whether to thank you for my promotion or throw you bodily out of my store for lying to me."

His eyes narrowed, but he didn't say anything.

"Of course it wouldn't be prudent to fire you now, would it?" Brandi mused. "So I guess I'll settle for thanking you for the recommendation you obviously gave me."

"I didn't have anything to do with your promotion, Brandi."

She hardly heard the denial because of the accompanying admission—that there was to be a promotion, and Zack quite obviously knew it. If he hadn't, he'd have said something else altogether. "Nothing at all?"

Zack shook his head. "It was Ross's decision. I didn't make any recommendation."

Brandi's voice was deceptively gentle. "You know, Zack, if you'd tell me the moon was shining, I'd go and check it out before I'd believe you."

He flushed a little, as if he felt ashamed.

"You've lied to me at every turn, and even when you've told the truth, it turned out to be a lie, too. You're a master of careful phrasing, aren't you? How dare you sit there in my office and say *there's nothing else I'd like to tell you*!"

"Brandi—"

She considered, for an instant, that it wasn't wise to say all this, that it would be better to keep her feelings inside and never let him see. But hurt and fury and disappointment welled up in her like an oil gusher, and once the surface calm had cracked, there was no stopping the flow.

"I suppose you believe the end justifies the means, Zack? Well, no matter how thrilled I am with my promotion, I think the way you conducted yourself is a disgrace. I can't ask you never to set foot in this store again, but I can promise that any further conversation between us will be limited to business. And I thank heaven it's only ten more days till Christmas, so you can get out of that ridiculous Santa suit and go back to playing with toys yourself. Have I made myself perfectly clear?"

"Oh, yes." Zack's voice had a hard edge to it. "And considering the circumstances, I can't imagine wanting to talk to you about anything. Will a handwritten resignation letter do, or shall I go over to electronics and type one?"

"Unless you're planning to give it to Ross, don't bother," Brandi snapped. "You've certainly never answered to me, and I wouldn't want you to pretend to start now!"

She turned on her heel and stalked off across Toyland.

At least that was all over, she told herself when she reached the safety of her office. It was finished. She didn't have to be concerned about Zack anymore, and she could relax and enjoy the challenge of her new promotion.

As soon as her head stopped aching.

The week edged by, and Brandi didn't hear from Ross. There wasn't even a phone call, much less an offer of a promotion.

After a couple of days of silence, she considered the possibility that Whitney's information might have been wrong. But she soon dismissed the idea. Zack had known about the promotion offer, too. It was real—or at least it had been at the time.

Of course, it was quite possible that after her explosion Zack had reconsidered his recommendation. He might well have gone back to Ross to report that Brandi Ogilvie was an uncontrollable maniac, unfit even for the position she already had, and completely unsuitable for anything higher.

Brandi thought that over and decided she didn't care. If the price of telling Zack exactly what she thought of him turned out to be the sacrifice of a job, then she was willing to accept the loss. At least she'd been honest. She could live without the job, and there would be another promotion someday—one she didn't owe to Zack Forrest.

In the meantime, she split her days between the store and the Wishing Tree. Someone had to take over, since Zack had walked away and Pat Emerson's flu was proving to be worse than the average case.

Actually, however, Zack hadn't quite walked away. He'd left a telephone message for her the day after he left the store, asking her to let him know if he was still needed to finish up the Wishing Tree. Brandi had asked Dora to call and tell him no.

She was surprised to find that she really enjoyed working on the Wishing Tree. Sorting through the requests, matching up the gifts that customers brought in, and making sure that every person on the tree was remembered was a detailed and time-consuming task, but it absorbed her attention in a way nothing else seemed to. Sometimes it hurt, though; every time Brandi looked at an application that displayed Zack's signature approving it, she felt as if she'd been stabbed anew.

To escape the paperwork, she started shopping for the family she'd adopted—the one she'd signed up on that Sunday afternoon when she'd first challenged Zack for the truth. Warm clothes for the children were easy enough, but shopping for the mother was difficult—what did one buy a woman whose only request had been for her children? And toys gave her a problem, too. She wasn't sure what to buy for boys.

More than once she found herself wishing that Zack was still around to ask. When that happened, she gritted her teeth and plunged back into work again.

She was in ladies' active wear one afternoon, looking at a casual slacks-and-sweater set and wondering if she could guess the size the woman wore, when Theresa Howard finished with another customer and came up to Brandi.

"That's a nice combination," Theresa said.

Brandi held up the sweater. "Do I hear a little hesitation in your voice?"

"Oh, no. But is it for you? I think the blues would show off your gorgeous hair better than pink would. May I show you?"

Brandi laughed. "Very tactful," she complimented. "You're obviously taking to this job. Actually, this is a gift."

Theresa relaxed. "Oh, in that case..." She was ringing up the sale when she added, "If you need help delivering all the Wishing Tree stuff, I'd be happy to volunteer. I'm still trying to get on my feet financially, so I can't donate much money, but I'd like to give something back, and I thought perhaps if I helped with deliveries..."

"I *will* need help, thank you." Brandi picked up the neatly bagged sweater and slacks. "I believe I mentioned right at the outset that this was probably just a seasonal job, Theresa?''

''Yes, ma'am. And I understand that, I really—''

Brandi interrupted. ''I've been talking with Miss Amos about your performance, and we've agreed that you can consider this position permanent.''

Theresa's eyes filled with tears. ''Oh, Ms. Ogilvie...''

''Unless, of course, you leave it to move up,'' Brandi added hastily, before she could start crying herself. ''And don't thank me, because you've earned it.''

Besides, she thought as she walked away, tucking the bag under her arm, if there was anyone who deserved Theresa Howard's thanks, it was Zack.

That reminded her of the snowy night in the parking lot and the first time Zack had kissed her, and she had to bite her lip hard to drown out the pain in her heart.

When she returned to her office, Ross Clayton rose from the chair beside Dora's desk. ''Finishing up your shopping?'' he asked cheerfully.

Brandi stared at him in surprise. It had been days since Whitney had told her of the promotion, since her confrontation with Zack. What was Ross doing here now? ''This is the last of it,'' she admitted, and ushered him into her office. She put the bag on the corner of her desk, so she wouldn't forget to wrap it to match the rest of the toys and clothes she'd bought for her Wishing Tree family, and sat down.

''I'm sorry it's taken me so long to get back to you,'' Ross said. He pulled up a chair across from her. ''I've been out of town, sorting out some trouble in the Phoenix store. That's a good deal of what I wanted to chat with you about. I need someone to do that job for me.''

Brandi's head was swimming. Did this mean the job offer was still good? But after the way she'd yelled at Zack...

Ross said, "You've talked to Whitney, no doubt?" Brandi nodded, and he smiled. "I knew I could count on her to pass the word along. What about it, Brandi? Are you interested in being my troubleshooter?"

Brandi looked down at her hands. Of course I'm interested, she thought. This was what she'd worked for since the very first week she'd been a salesclerk, when she'd set her sights on a much higher goal. She was going to have a career, not a job that simply let her get by....

"I think you're ideally qualified," Ross went on, "because you're not only experienced at the store level, but you're bright and you're a creative problem solver. But I won't sugarcoat this offer—it wouldn't be fair. This isn't an easy or a popular job."

"I've always liked challenges, and I've never worried about being popular." But Brandi's voice sounded odd to her own ears, as if it belonged to someone else.

Ross leaned back in his chair as if confident that he had his answer. "The thing that convinced me, you know, was when you sniffed Zack out. There was no reason to think his being here had anything to do with you—but you knew it. That's exactly the kind of sixth sense I'm looking for."

Brandi didn't think it was necessary to tell him that that hadn't been her managerial instincts at work, but an awareness of an entirely different sort. *My nose for trouble*, she told herself, aware that wasn't quite true, either.

"I can't legally ask you whether you plan to stay single," Ross went on, "but I must warn you that this kind of job is terribly hard on families and friendships."

Brandi closed her eyes, and once more let an image wash over her, of two small children and a train and a Christmas tree...and Zack. The scene was faded now, as if it was a photograph that had been left out in the sun, but it still had the power to move her.

"You can plan to be on the road up to six weeks at a time," Ross said, "and away from home about fifty weeks of the year. If you want to try it, I would like to have a commitment from you for two years in this job. After that, we'll talk about what you want to do next. Maybe move through the district managers' positions, getting to know the whole chain."

She took a deep breath and wondered why she wasn't happier. Certainly he was not making the job sound like a plum, but that was no surprise; Ross wasn't the kind to hide the disadvantages of whatever he offered. Brandi had known about the difficulties of the job anyway, so why was she reacting now as if they were insuperable? Why did she have this nagging feeling, now that the plum lay within her reach, that she really didn't want it after all?

She was being stupid, she told herself. Zack would never be a part of her life. The children she had once visualized so clearly were nothing more than a wispy dream. She was free as a cloud, responsible only to herself. And *for* herself. Certainly for the sake of her future, it would be wise to take the promotion. And yet...

Her gaze fell on the blue-and-silver paisley bag that lay on the corner of her desk. She wanted to take the necessary time to wrap that package as beautifully as she could. She wanted to be there to watch as it was opened, and perhaps to get to know that woman better.

She wanted to watch Theresa Howard grow in confidence, move up in the department, maybe eventually take it over after Casey Amos left.

She couldn't do those things if she took the job Ross offered, for she would not be able to stay in one place long enough to nurture a friendship. Not as the troubleshooter. And probably not afterward, either, if she had to move around the country in order to continue up the corporate ladder.

Perhaps she wasn't as free as she'd believed. Perhaps her treasured independence had truly been self-imposed isolation instead.

A year or two ago, she wouldn't have given a second thought to leaving everything and everyone behind for a new challenge. Now, without even realizing it, she had grown roots here.

"If you'd like a chance to think it over before giving me an answer..." Ross began.

Brandi shook her head, almost automatically. "No. I can answer you now." She wet her lips and said, "Thanks, Ross, but I'm happy where I am."

He was obviously startled. "Perhaps I shouldn't have hit you with this in the midst of the busiest season. Take a while to think, Brandi. After Christmas is over and things settle down a bit, you may change your mind."

"It won't make a difference," she warned.

He studied her thoughtfully for a moment, and then his eyes began to sparkle. "I see. My wife and Whitney both said there was something cooking between you and Zack—"

Brandi said steadily, "This has nothing to do with Zack. It's just what's best for me."

Ross gave her a knowing grin.

Obviously he didn't understand, Brandi thought. But then, she hadn't expected him to.

* * *

The employee party was always held on the last Sunday before Christmas, starting just after the store closed. There had been a an air or excitement all afternoon; Brandi caught the drifts of enthusiasm as she walked through the store shortly before closing time. She even caught herself humming a snatch of "Jingle Bells" once.

She wasn't precisely happy, of course. She thought it would probably be a long time before the ache in her heart receded enough to be ignored, and she didn't even dream of a day when she might altogether forget the twin agonies of loving Zack and discovering his lies.

But there were increasing stretches of time when she was content, for she was certain the decision to stay at the store was the right one.

She'd done as Ross asked; she'd spent many hours thinking about the job he'd offered. Sometimes, in the darkest hours of the night, she'd found herself thinking that perhaps she *should* take it. In the troubleshooter's post she could get away from almost everything and make a fresh start.

But that was the problem, Brandi concluded. The things she *could* leave behind, she didn't particularly want to. And the memory of Zack—the one thing she'd have liked to forget—would accompany her no matter where she went or what she did.

By the time she got downstairs to the party, the store was officially closed, the caterers had set up the long buffet tables in the atrium, and stacks of brightly wrapped packages of all sizes were appearing under the largest of the Christmas trees.

Brandi slid the package she'd brought into the nearest stack as discreetly as she could. As she turned away from the tree, she ran headlong into Casey Amos, who hunched protectively over the packages she carried. Her eyes widened when she saw Brandi.

Brandi shook a playful finger at her. "You look guilty," she chided. "I'll bet you took an extralong coffee break this afternoon to wrap those, didn't you? Shame."

Casey swallowed hard. "You want some shrimp?" she said weakly. "Let me get rid of these and I'll join you."

The caterer's table was a masterpiece, loaded with simple food beautifully arranged to tempt the palate. Brandi picked up a plate and pulled a giant boiled shrimp off a lettuce-wrapped stand.

From the corner of her eye, she caught a glimpse of a red velvet suit, and her heart seemed to do a somersault. Don't be silly, she thought. In the first place, Zack couldn't possibly be attending the employees' party, because he wasn't an employee anymore. In the second place, he certainly wouldn't be wearing a Santa suit.

Very deliberately, she turned around to prove to herself that the suspicion was only a figment of her imagination, and discovered that she'd been half-right. The Santa she'd seen was the one with the half glasses, who hadn't bothered to change clothes after his shift.

Zack wasn't wearing red velvet.

He was standing at the entrance. His black-and-white patterned sweater seemed to Brandi's eyes to swirl like an optical illusion, and she thought for a moment that she was going to faint.

She had convinced herself that she was better, that the agony was receding, that someday soon she would forget him. Now she knew how foolish she had been. She had been hiding from the pain, but seeing him again brought it all bubbling up like an acid bath. And she had to admit that she would never be all right, that she would never forget, and that she missed him more than she had thought it possible to long for another human being.

She had thought she loved Jason, and time had salved the wound. But this was different. This was forever.

Beside her, Casey Amos heaved a long sigh, as if she'd made up her mind about something desperate. "I'd better confess."

"What?" Brandi said tersely. "That you invited Zack?"

"Is he here?" Casey looked over her shoulder, only half-interested. "No, it's not that. I hope you won't hate me, but I put your name in the gift exchange drawing."

"Is that all?"

"I thought it was too bad for you not to be included. But it hit me when I saw you putting a package into the pile a minute ago that you'll be the only employee to get two gifts tonight."

A couple of weeks ago Brandi would have been a bit annoyed at being dragged into something she had no interest in. As it was, she thought the mix-up was mildly funny; she'd probably be teased for a day or two and then the event would be forgotten. "Don't worry about it, Casey. I just hope you got something nice for the person whose name I'm supposed to have drawn in return." Her gaze drifted toward Zack once more; he'd moved toward the Christmas tree.

Across the serving table, Theresa Howard turned pale and dropped a shrimp. "I put your name in, too," she whispered. "Casey said something about your being left out, and I thought..."

The humor of the situation—and the rightness of the decision she'd made—struck Brandi sharply, and she started to laugh uncontrollably. "What a party," she managed to say finally. "I wouldn't have missed this for the world!"

Even if Zack *was* there, for he stayed at the fringes of the crowd. Brandi had started to relax, thinking that he was as intent on avoiding her as she was on staying out of his way, when they abruptly came face-to-face at the portable bar.

"How's business?" Brandi asked, trying to keep her voice light. She squeezed the twist of lime into her club soda and wiped her fingertips on a napkin.

"Busy. We're reorganizing produce lines, repackaging some toys in smaller units... nothing earthshaking in itself, but I hope it will have an impact well before next Christmas season."

"I'm sure it will." She didn't look directly at him. "I'm happy you found what was wrong."

For a moment, she thought he wasn't going to answer. Then he said softly, "And I'm happy you're getting the job you want."

Before Brandi could tell him any differently, he'd walked away. Not that it mattered, she thought. But the ache in the pit of her stomach—the nagging pain that had been her constant companion since the day she'd found out he'd spied on her—intensified.

The gift exchange proceeded with more than usual hilarity; Brandi's three packages got exactly the reaction she'd expected. Then a fourth was delivered, and she laughingly demanded, "All right. I know about Casey and Theresa, but who else has been setting me up?" Too late, she looked across the circle at Zack. He, too, had thought she was a Scrooge who needed a dose of Christmas spirit....

Dora sheepishly raised a hand, and also the manager of Toyland, who said, "I thought it would be sad if you weren't included on your last Christmas—" He caught himself too late and clapped a hand over his mouth.

Brandi sighed. Obviously Whitney had been right about the corporate grapevine. Too bad the gossips hadn't picked up on the latest installment. "No, I'm not terminally ill," she said over the speculative whispers.

"And no matter what rumor says, I'm not leaving to take another job, either." She looked down at the stack of gifts in her lap. They were small things, even silly things, but the thought that had gone into them meant a great deal to her. "I'm happy here—with my friends." It was mostly true, she told herself. She was as happy as she could be just now.

The party ended early, since they were going into the final and most wearing week of the season. Zack left among the first group, walking out with Theresa Howard. Brandi tried not to notice. She stayed till the caterers had cleaned up the last scrap of turkey, and then she locked the employee exit behind her and went home.

Another ordeal survived, she told herself. It would get easier with time, though she could no longer fool herself that the pain would end entirely someday.

She made a hollow in the garland on the mantel so she could set up one of her gifts there—a ceramic statuette of a winking Santa—and she was just setting him in place when the doorbell rang. Through the peephole, she recognized Zack, and with resignation she opened the door.

"I'm glad you didn't pretend not to be home," he said. "I'd have looked pretty silly climbing up the drainpipe and over the balcony rail."

Brandi didn't invite him in, but leaned against the jamb with the door open only a few inches. "I can't see why that would be necessary. If you left something at the party, you can get it at the store tomorrow. I'm not going back tonight."

Zack shook his head. "That's not why I'm here. Didn't Ross come through with the job offer?"

"Why not ask him? I suppose you're worried because you recommended me and I didn't live up to expectations."

Zack looked exasperated. "Look, must we have this conversation with my foot in the door?"

"I didn't invite you here."

"Brandi, I don't blame you for being angry with me. And I'm not justifying what I did. But I'd like to have a chance to explain it—so you'll know I didn't do it for fun, or without thinking it through."

Brandi shrugged and moved back from the door. "I suppose I have nothing to lose by listening."

She purposely didn't offer him a cup of coffee, and she didn't sit down. Zack didn't seem to notice; he moved around her living room with the nervous energy of a caged panther, stopping for a moment to look at the ceramic Santa on the mantel. Brandi had forgotten that, or she'd have left him standing in the hall.

"Ross and I have been friends since college days," Zack began. "In fact, we met in the dean's office—both of us were close to being thrown out of school because of a little too much high-spirited fun. Ever since then, we've pitched in to help each other when trouble's brewing, so of course when I started getting bad news about my Christmas sales, I called Ross."

Brandi decided to hurry things along. "And he thought it would be a good idea to kill two birds with one stone by sending you to spy on me."

Zack winced. "He didn't, Brandi. All he asked of me was an opinion about how well you'd be suited to the job he was thinking of offering you."

"That's what I called it," Brandi said softly. "Spying."

"No. He was just asking for another point of view— it's the kind of thing I've done myself a thousand times, with Ross and with others. He knew you were good, you see—that was never in doubt. But he questioned whether you were flexible enough for the fast changes and the constant shifts that a troubleshooter faces every day. All he wanted was an opinion. The decision would be his, no matter what I thought.''

She shrugged. That must be what he meant when he said he hadn't actually made a recommendation. It ended up being the same thing.

"It seemed a very small favor," Zack said softly, "compared to the one he was doing for me, so I agreed. I didn't realize then—how could I, Brandi?—that it wasn't just Ross's employee I'd be looking at.'' Zack was looking very steadily at her. "I had no idea that I was going to meet a very special woman here."

Brandi swallowed hard. *A very special woman.* It wasn't all she wanted; in fact, it wasn't really very much at all, but she would treasure those words forever. It was half a minute—an achingly long silence—before she regained her balance enough to say coolly, "That's touching, Zack. But once that possibility occurred to you, didn't you think about backing out of your promise and telling me what was going on?"

"Yes—but don't forget that by the time I realized I needed to tell you the truth, I was in pretty deep. I warned Ross the night of the party that I was going to tell you the whole thing—my reasons for masquerading as Santa, the troubleshooter job..."

Brandi's body went absolutely still. He had intended to confess the whole lot?

"And I tried," Zack went on softly, "but you ran away rather than listen to me. The next day, when you found out about Intellitoys, you didn't even try to understand that there might have been a reason for not telling you right away. You didn't ask questions. You just attacked."

I was hurt, she wanted to say. I was aching with love for you, and you didn't even seem to care that I might have liked to know what was going on! "I suppose that's why you didn't make a recommendation to Ross, because I'd conducted myself so badly. Why didn't you just tell him I'd be a terrible troubleshooter?"

She thought for a moment he wasn't going to answer. Then he said quietly, "Because I thought you'd make a damned good one."

A very special woman . . . She felt as if he'd snatched away the fragment of joy that comment had held for her; obviously he'd meant it professionally, not personally, after all. She ought to have known that from the beginning.

"Even after that I wanted to confess it all," Zack said, "and at least be square with you, whatever else happened. But don't you see, Brandi? If I told you what Ross was considering, and you changed your behavior in the least—as you'd be bound to do, it's only human—he would never have offered you the job. I was caught in my own trap."

She nodded a little.

"So I told Ross I couldn't make a recommendation, that I was too personally interested in you to have a valid opinion."

"And he believed that?" Brandi's voice was dry. Then she remembered what Ross had said about his wife's suspicions, and Whitney's. Maybe Ross *had* believed it.

"Any reason he shouldn't?" Zack sounded a little annoyed. "Just because you can't stand having me around—"

Brandi's heart seemed to give a sudden jolt and stop beating altogether. "What did you say?"

"Look, you've made it obvious how you feel, Brandi. Your career comes first, and I respect that. I don't have much choice about it, do I?" He zipped his leather jacket. "All right, I've said what I came to say. At least you know I didn't lie to you for the sheer enjoyment of it, so I won't bother you anymore."

As he brushed past her, Brandi's hand grasped his sleeve. The contact seemed to burn her fingers, and Zack stopped as if he'd run into an electrical field.

Brandi stared up at him, willing him to stay, knowing that if he left she would always regret letting him go. Her fingers tightened.

Slowly his hand closed over hers and tugged it loose. But instead of letting her go, he cradled her fingers on his, and ever so slowly raised her hand to his face.

She let her fingers curve around his jaw, savoring the warmth of him and the faintest prickle of his beard. If she could never touch him again, she thought, she would treasure this moment, this memory. She smiled just a little, and her eyes misted, and so she couldn't see clearly what emotion was in his face as he pulled her tightly against him.

He kissed her as if he couldn't deny himself, and his hunger woke a passion in her that was deeper than anything Brandi had ever felt before. This is where I belong, she thought, and burrowed against him as if she was trying to make herself a part of his body.

Eventually he stopped kissing her and simply cradled her close, his cheek against her hair. "Dammit, Brandi," he said unsteadily, "you're not my kind of woman."

Slowly, sanity dawned. Brandi tried to pull away from him, embarrassed at her own uninhibited behavior.

But Zack wouldn't let her go. "I've always made it a point to steer clear of high-powered career types."

"Love 'em and leave 'em," she said coolly, remembering what Whitney had said.

"No," Zack corrected. "Have fun, but don't get serious. And I planned to do the same with you. But it just didn't work, you see." A note of bitter humor crept into his voice. "I came here tonight to confess—so I might as well tell it all, right? I didn't realize right away why you affected me so. I thought for days that I was always on edge around you because I didn't like you at all."

"Gee, thanks." The crack in Brandi's voice robbed the comment of irony.

"The night you asked me if I was Ross's trouble-shooter... You were so vulnerable, so helpless, so open, and I began to think that you might be what I'd been looking for all these years. It was almost a heretical thought—that my idea of the perfect woman had been so far from the reality. But then at the party, I saw you with the kids—and I couldn't help but think that you wanted that, too. I guess it was wishful thinking, wasn't it?"

Brandi's throat was tight with pain and unshed tears.

"I was going to propose to you that night," Zack said softly. "And then—if you accepted me—I planned to throw myself at your feet and tell you the truth."

She'd asked him what he was going to tell her that night, and he'd dodged the question instead of answering—and so she'd assumed he'd intended to share only a version of the truth. How could she have been so blind?

"But you wouldn't stick around to listen. The only thing I could think was that you knew what I wanted to say—and you didn't want to have to turn me down, so it was easier to run away than to hear me out."

Brandi put her hand to her temple, where a vein throbbed.

"I knew then I'd read you wrong after all, that your career was more important than I could ever be. And I loved you so much I wanted you to have what you wanted—even if it wasn't me." He kissed her hair gently, and set her aside. "It isn't too late, I'm sure. I'll talk to Ross—"

Brandi had to clear her throat twice before she could say, "He offered me the job. I turned it down, Zack."

He stood as if turned to stone. "What?"

"Why do you think I blew up at you like that? I didn't do it on purpose, exactly, but I thought if I exploded at you, you'd tell Ross I shouldn't get the job."

"You *wanted* that to happen?"

"I didn't reason it out ahead of time. But yes, I think I did."

"Why don't you want the job?" He sounded as if he'd been hit a solid blow just beneath the ribs.

Brandi didn't look at him. She picked out a spot on the front of his jacket instead and stared at it. "A long time ago, I thought I was in love," she said slowly. "He was a charming man, but he liked things easy—so when he found a woman who had family money, he dumped me. And I decided never to let anyone get that close to me again. Especially not the happy-go-lucky sort who didn't worry about where the next car payment was coming from—"

"And who'd take a temporary job as Santa Claus to make ends meet? I think I begin to see."

She nodded. "I wasn't looking for a man at all, but even if I had been, you were so obviously not what I wanted that it never occurred to me to be wary of you. But before I realized what had happened, you'd crept into my heart—and made me want to feel again, and to give, and to be close to people. . . ."

Zack drew her tightly against him once more. He kissed her temple, and the pain went away. But there was still a knot in her stomach. "I love you. But I don't know, Zack," she said on a rising note of panic. "I'm scared. Kids are so important to you. What if I can't be a good mother? I'm not exactly promising parent material!''

He smiled down at her. ''If you weren't,'' he said softly, ''it would never occur to you to ask the question. We'll wait till you're ready, that's all. And if you're never ready, I can live with that—as long as I have you.''

Slowly, the knot eased. ''You scare me to death sometimes,'' she confessed, ''but I've never been as alive as when I'm with you.''

''Can you forgive me for not being completely truthful with you?''

Brandi nodded. ''Now I can. Now that I understand why.''

He kissed her again; it was as much a promise as a caress. ''If you still want the job, Brandi, we'll make it work somehow.''

She considered the question, and shook her head. ''My career is important to me, Zack. But it's not all-important anymore.''

Zack's hands slid slowly down her back, drawing her even closer against him. ''And what *is* all-important?''

Brandi looked up into his eyes, and the last whisper of doubt disappeared. This was right, and real, and forever. ''You are,'' she confessed. ''And you always will be—my unlikely Santa.''

If you are looking for more titles by

LEIGH MICHAELS

Don't miss these fabulous stories by one of
Harlequin's most renowned authors:

(limited quantities available on certain titles)

TOTAL AMOUNT	$
POSTAGE & HANDLING	$
($1.00 for one book, 50¢ for each additional)	
APPLICABLE TAXES*	$
TOTAL PAYABLE	$

(check or money order—please do not send cash)

To order, complete this form and send it, along with a check or money order
for the total above, payable to Harlequin Books, to: **In the U.S.:** 3010 Walden
Avenue, P.O. Box 9047, Buffalo, NY 14269-9047; **In Canada:** P.O. Box 613,
Fort Erie, Ontario, L2A 5X3.

Name: _____

Address: _____ City: _____

State/Prov.: _____ Zip/Postal Code: _____

*New York residents remit applicable sales taxes.
 Canadian residents remit applicable GST and provincial taxes.   HLMBACK4

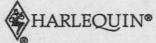

HARLEQUIN®

MILLION DOLLAR SWEEPSTAKES (III)

EXTRA BONUS PRIZE DRAWING

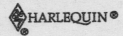